BALDING

JEFFREY ELLINGER

To those who have suffered

JEFFREY ELLINGER

"…It is not good for the man to be alone…" - Genesis 2:18

I

Sing, Goddess, of doing nothing and
hating yourself, of melodramatic
beginnings to self-published novels, of a
dark-haired Parisian nymphet reading
The Loser and hearing the buzzing
beneath, of watching her breasts jostle
beneath a shimmering black blouse with
gold trim, of wanting her and never
having her or anyone else, of bewailing
the day we could have gone down
another path and learned a romance
language for her at least, of dying when
she switches effortlessly to English to
swear, of listening to her talk about how
sweaty she has become, of watching
her until the pain in our gut becomes
pleasurable, of turning to salt when we
see her kiss another on social media, of
eating the grass and dying in a ditch
where the brown water collects and
dead leaves rot, of stealing from
classics, of worry and sadness.

Tell, Muse, of single media types in New
York City, of how I am damned to
eternal burning for thinking I should
shrink myself down to miniature size to
live inside them. Muse, do not forget as I
lament my lot as a narrator who cannot
get out of his head. Please become a
primitive doctor and drive out the bad
humors and biles. Take me to Iowa,

JEFFREY ELLINGER

where I can grow like a cornstalk out of
the black earth speckled with white
spots of rich fertilizer like the kief they
smoke in Brooklyn after they have gone
to Iowa to write made-up stories and
learned there is no money in writing
made-up stories and have become the
single media types of my dreams.

Lie, Satan, about how many words we
know, about how many backsides we
have spanked, about how many inches
we have grown, about the age spots not
showing up on our hands, about the hair
not sprouting on our knuckles, about the
guy in the next cubicle who sounds like
he is whittling wood or eating a very
crunchy cereal, about a love story that is
a cross between *Scenes from a
Marriage* and *Pauline at the Beach*
starring Milo and Roxane, about getting
us to care enough to write that story,
about how many tweets there are.

Flail, Human, punching keys in vain
hoping to be noticed, pushing a rock up
a hill every day only to have that rock
fall back down every night and then to
wake up every morning to push it back
up, using the word "Sisyphean"
correctly, saying other words to other
humans as if they cared to hear words
that are not their own words or the

words of humans they are attracted to
telling them to bare the parts they most
want to lick, going to a job to acquire
money to buy more food to give the
energy to go to a job to buy more food,
immersing yourself in old books as if
anyone read anything other than the
latest news about nuclear war and
sexual harassers, to be different than
what you came out of the womb as,
wandering around in nature, death.

Eradicate, Mother, swipe us from the
face of the earth. Do not spare a single
one. We have done harm with our
pathetic yearnings and metal engines.
Mother, ease our feeble pain. Delete us
from the earth. Erase the internet. Dig
up the underground wires and in their
place grow useful plants and another
Adam and Eve. Place them in the
Garden. Adam has a big floppy penis
and Eve has the most pert breasts and
a perfect bush and the kind of butt
attached to thick thighs that is kind of
like one big muscle. Do not delay,
Mother: we are at the end, pretending
we are good but torn up inside thinking
of our mistakes. Mother, send the flood.
Talk to the Goddess, the Muse, and
Satan, but do not listen to the Human,
who is filth and genocide. Speak not of
mercy, for we are debased. This is only

a way to stall before we go back to
work.

Give me the energy, Lord, to be a strong
beautiful black woman who is not in
need of a man. You created everything
and existed before anything and made a
ball of infinite energy. After You made
that ball You watched as it imploded,
and what a ruckus. Zing. Zoom.
Whoosh. The rocks and waters flew in
every direction. Quite the sight, but only
You were there to see. In the beginning
You embodied every particle and got a
feel for every possible thing so now You
know what it's like to be a cell inside of
an atom inside of a piece of dirt. You
also know what it's like to be blackness
in space, and to be the tip of a penis of
a blue whale on Your favorite of all the
creations, what You named Earth. On
Earth You took time to separate land
from water and day from night and You
put creatures in the sea and more on
land, and for a good long while You just
were, thinking of how one day You
would murder everyone with a flood and
also create a rival so You could blame
someone else for pestilence and
disease and evil so vile it is too much for
You to watch.

In the beginning You focused on Paul Bethel and the ways You could impede his development. Out the womb You gave him an oblong head. This was around the time a film was released about an alien with an oblong head, a movie that took eons to be made, from Your perspective, and yet right as Paul Bethel entered elementary school that movie became popular. What cruel timing, but You were happy and gave Paul enough softness to ensure he would have galvanizing experiences upon which he would later reflect, purging them from his body by writing what he called fiction and later self-publishing those so-called fictions and gnashing his teeth when no one recognized his work. You gave Paul a heart desirous of a girlfriend and true love---as if he were a Renaissance poet or an eighteenth-century French musketeer---and placed him in the Middle West of a continent, far away from the highest densities of potential mates on either coast, where he could have networked with connected individuals, like publishers who would want this story about how the world began. You gave Paul a lisp that led to being bullied which led to journaling in college which led into searching for truth which led him to believe there was only one soul on this planet who You

9

arranged for him. Paul based that idea on a book called *I Hugged Courtship Hello*, written by a teenager from Oregon who said that a man and woman should not touch or kiss one another until the day of their marriage. Paul believed in that teen's book and toiled for years to find ordained love, until he came upon the idea to write the story of how everything began. And while You knew no one else would read Paul's story before You let go of the ball of infinite energy, You did not stop Paul as You held it—You liked to experience everything—and also You thought of everything else, like what it would be like for Paul to sit at his desk in his cubicle, his eye twitching from a morning spent worrying that he hadn't tipped enough for his coffee and croissant and would lose more hair as punishment. By the time of that twitching You had seen inside every worm and every piece of iron and every teen praise and worship leader with tan breasts pushed together and every single thing that ever was or would be.

Long after the creation of everything Paul Bethel was born in Sioux Falls, South Dakota. In childhood, Paul played a part in a few events which may have been worthy of recording, if anyone beyond Paul had cared to record them.

This narrator is aware, at least, of a couple of no-hitters thrown in little league, feats that seem more like a dream to Paul with each passing year. In high school, Paul made out with a cheerleader from a neighboring school after an away basketball game, and again in the Corn Palace after the regional basketball tournament his senior year, but because he had no idea how those kisses happened—and was unable to convince his friends they did— those tender moments began to be forgotten. Uninterested in farming like his father, after high school Paul attended the state university's college of agriculture and fell in love with God, which exemplifies the way Paul Bethel made decisions: poorly, and with a knack for bad timing. College for Paul would be a period of strict boundaries. At the end of his freshman year he wrote a binding contract on loose-leaf paper—after a terrifying brush with sex—pledging to not drink, to not do drugs, and, the most important commandment, to not touch a woman until marriage. Paul prayed every day for her, but she never appeared in those four years, so Paul left a virgin. After graduation he went to Alaska, and to go that far north, Paul believed, would give him something he could later recite

when asked by a sister in Christ: Where
have you been? What have you done?

Well, he could say to her—the one God
handpicked from the trillions of humans
to ever exist, after a raucous service at
a nondenominational church—every
morning when I woke up I could see
mountains, and mountains beyond
mountains. What God made is so
beautiful, don't you think?

Dreams of flirtatious beginnings filled
Paul's head as he worked in the Yukon
Valley, riding on horseback and hauling
big game carcasses to a base camp
where he cleaned the animals that the
businessmen, rich as pharaohs, had
killed. The job, Paul told his family,
would be a summer thing, though he
secretly harbored the possibility of
moving up to the unforgiving land for
good. Problem was, Paul could never be
an outdoorsman, no matter how much
he tried. He liked having an Arby's close
by, and a Blockbuster, and there was
always the pull of something invisible
waiting for him in some great metropolis,
as if the average lot Paul had been born
into was a mistake, like a mix-up at the
factory.

The summer of youth went by, and after the job Paul stayed in Alaska for a weekend of reflections on singledom. One night in his meager hotel room he daydreamed of hitching his way up the coast. He had heard a man could fish on commercial vessels. Wilderness loomed as Paul walked around and around the same city block, reminded of the time when as a little boy he got sick on a tour of Lake Michigan. As the choppy water crashed against the boat, Paul sat still on his mother's lap and chewed green spearmint gum, given to him by a kind Chicagoan in the seat directly ahead. As a man, Paul looked out at the jagged terrain and the portentous waters and hoped the sea wouldn't affect him like it once did. Later that evening, Paul ran the idea by his family, and Dad did not like it. Not because of the seasickness in his son, but because Paul's father would never believe Paul could do any better in any other state, or in any other city, which were the only places Paul thought he could do better. In some disgust, Dad handed the phone over to Mom.

Now Pauly, she said before her mouth reached the receiver. Don't you remember that time in Chicago? Don't you remember how sick you got?

JEFFREY ELLINGER

Paul had known she would mention
Chicago, but this far away, he had to let
her speak her mind. And he couldn't lie.
He remembered it well. But I didn't
throw up, he said, did I?

Oh, I don't know if you threw up, Paul,
but why would you want to chance
something like that? Ya know, once
you're on a boat like that you're not
getting off. I think you should be sure
about this.

Not sure of anything, Paul tried to
convey to his parents that he was
making the right decision, and that he
wasn't like the boy they knew, the one
who couldn't make up his mind. But the
very next day, after another aimless
walk, Paul decided he would go home. It
wasn't really a decision so much as a
settling into the path of least resistance,
and as Paul packed up he reminded
himself how hard it was to sleep, *what
with all the light up here*. This wasn't
quitting, just being practical. Perhaps,
though, perhaps, Paul thought in his
seat on the plane, next to a man with a
rugged face who kept coughing,
perhaps there were too many directions
that seemed viable. Air shot from the
blower, like the breath of God saying:

Go home, figure things out there. At home, one can make a permanent decision.

The flight would be like the two other flights Paul had taken so far in life. He tried to sleep, and as soon as he managed it he'd wake to drool running from his cheek to form a slimy pool on his shoulder. After another cough woke him, Paul wiped off the wetness and took out a book on the Romans in the time of Christ. What good is it to read something made up? This is what Paul would have said at the time, agreeing with others who faithfully read books on finding a partner for marriage and other, even more enriching books on the historical findings of the Resurrection. Those books armed men with the conversational ammunition to bring people into a relationship with Jesus. They were necessary and edifying. The book on Paul's lap looked solid, and as he read he evaluated the words as interesting and knew if anyone asked him how the book was he'd say the same thing: It was interesting. He turned the page absently and left the possibly life-altering words behind. Through his small window the cramped view opened to a billowing mat of clouds, like the future spread before him.

JEFFREY ELLINGER

At home he and his friends talked about
the future, and that kind of suspended
life suited Paul fine. To talk of plans in
the comfort of home seemed much
easier than carrying them out. That's
how it went for a while, but at every turn
Mom, and more often Dad, would ask,
What's the plan? And Paul would squirm
his way out of a long talk by alluding to
some half-baked intention of applying to
a job he didn't want. The longer he
stayed, the more difficult that became.
To get breathing room, he moved in with
his sister and brother-in-law in Yankton.
That fall was hot and Paul spent most of
his time in their air-conditioned
basement, the concrete floor cooling his
feet while he looked for work. While on
the computer Paul had to try hard not to
click on titillating spam ads. If he gave in
to lust, it'd be weeks before he could
think straight again. Focusing on the
task at hand, Paul cast his job net close.
What the future held, he couldn't say,
but he had to go. Living under the same
roof as his sister and her husband was
not sustainable. Young and newly
married meant certain things, things
Paul couldn't help but assume went on
under the blanket they shared when
they watched movies on the couch. With
just a degree in psychology, his options
were limited, but Paul did not consider

himself hindered. He believed he could work wherever God sent him. That was his thinking, deep and true, and he had no reservations about expressing his beliefs to anyone who asked.

For all I care, Paul would proudly say, I could work at a car wash. As long as I'm bringing people to Christ, it's the right job.

Instead of a car wash, Paul would begin work at a ranch in Nebraska that corralled delinquent youths, bringing them back to the herd of good behavior and godliness. He learned from the headmaster that while the ranch did not have an explicit directive to convert the boys to Christianity, there was also no mandate disallowing it. Paul dreamed of combining the knowledge from his studies, what little he had, with his desires, helping people get to heaven. It was perfect, he thought, and he took the minimum-wage offer. Along with him to Nebraska Paul brought the essentials: his minimal wardrobe, a box of old letters from camp girlfriends, a photo album, and the Bible. Once there, he settled into his spartan surroundings knowing he would not find a wife, not in such a desolate place. Instead, Paul sensed, he'd found a land where he could make himself ready for one. After a couple months of breaking up fights between boys who'd been given a short straw, one of his high school classmates called.

Same girl, Ryan Kaufman was saying. The same girl, now a woman, Ryan had met at the Turner County Fair their sophomore year and married at the end of their senior year. Still living in Rapid, Ryan said. Been working with an electrician. Going through the apprenticeship program.

That's great, Paul said. Really great.

Yep, Sheena and I are renting a place, but pretty soon we'll be in the market to buy. Need a place for the little guy. He's cookin' right now. Should be out next month.

Oh wow. Wow, Ryan. That's great. And while Paul tried to sound happy, he was unsure if his voice betrayed his concern that a human being would grow inside of Ryan's wife, impregnated by a man who as a boy in the seventh grade stuck his hand down the front of his pants and smelled his fingers with deep breaths. The same Ryan who in the eighth grade held down a classmate and made her

smell that very hand. But that was long
ago, and Paul shook his head. Things
had to be different now. They were
grown.

What are you up to these days, Paul?

I'm down here in Nebraska, actually.

Nebraska? Why?

Yeah, well, I work at a ranch for kids
who've been in juvie, stuff like that. It's
good, but nothing like working in Alaska.

Alaska? Ryan said it in a disapproving
way, and for a second Paul worried that
his old classmate might revert to his
adolescent persona of bully. But without
the help of the other boys Ryan had
become powerless, feckless in
comparison to the Ramses he'd been in
puberty.

Just working, living, Paul said, with just
enough confidence. It was good. But I
think I'll stay around here for a while.
See what comes of it.

A hesitant silence followed, and it
seemed their conversation had come to
an end. They could have heard it in
each other's voices. Familiar before,

they had matured and become unknown. Nothing left now other than tedious updates. They couldn't begin to breach the barrier that kept them from talking about thoughts and emotions, the kinds of topics that could be considered real. So they said goodbye, and as Paul put the phone on the receiver he imagined Ryan going out to a white van—with spools of wire and mini-drawers of screws and fasteners—to learn how to be an electrician so he could do right by his wife and first child.

That must be a good feeling, Paul thought, to have that kind of purpose. Then again, with so much purpose an inevitable responsibility follows, and there was more life to live, so many people to meet, places to go. Going to bed that night, Paul convinced himself of something he couldn't articulate. A cold driving wind bashed against the wall, making the night seem more menacing than cozy. And on his single mattress, with orphan boys snoring in bunk beds nearby, Paul pictured Ryan's family: a pregnant wife nestling close to her husband, warm and comforted, with that day's problems assuaged by a sweet voice. How good that must be, Paul thought restlessly, how amazingly good. Eventually sleep came, but for the first

time in Paul Bethel's life it seemed
strange to do so alone.

—

What was next for the very smart and
handsome man, according to Paul's
mom, the sensitive one with all the
opportunities? Paul's chest hair had not
grown in, and he could not grow a
proper beard. The hair that would one
day sprout on his shoulders and back
lay dormant. He lived with a lithe body in
need of no upkeep, and he was in love.
That summer on the ranch Paul came
face to face with her, transcendence,
and all that emotion she brought up
must have made him even more foolish
than usual, as he had almost six months
of riding under his belt when he first
approached Emily Canton. Just alight
from his horse, she said with a glint in
her eye, So is that how they teach you
boys to ride in Dakota?

To Paul, Emily will always be wearing
blue jeans, in the winter or in the
squelching heat of summer. He will
always see, when he thinks of her, a
face that made him stand up straight
when she came to the ranch to care for
the horses and give the boys riding
lessons. Never did she take their guff.

JEFFREY ELLINGER

Paul cannot remember them snickering about Emily having a real tight ass, as they would say under their breath about other women who came to the ranch. There was something about Emily that said she would not put up with that kind of lawlessness. It could have been her yellow-blonde hair—always tied in a braid—or her unshakeable good posture. Whatever it was, because of the boys' timidity around her, Paul could never demonstrate his manliness in the way he wanted. And demonstrating his manliness was important to Paul. Emily didn't seem to have a boyfriend.

One still evening after the boys had gone to bed, Paul and Emily finished the chores. Paul assisted Emily in the stables, wondering what their life together might be like. All he knew is that they would have a permanent address, so that when it came time to send Christmas cards to the Bethel home no one would have to worry about getting it wrong. In college, Paul overheard a guy on the campus radio say: Women don't want to be your savior. Paul had to suppress the urge to deify Emily as she helped him start a campfire. They sat on logs and talked. Paul couldn't have asked for more.

You're such a city boy, Emily was
saying. She stoked the fire in a way that
seemed intimate to Paul. I could tell the
first time I saw you.

Sioux Falls really isn't that big, Paul
said. I'm from the country, when you
think about it.

But you said you don't like country
music, Emily said. Her bangs were
curly. Her makeup gave her face a
mauve hue. Doesn't everybody from
South Dakota like country music?

I do, he said. I just like the old stuff.
Johnny Cash, Dolly Parton, that stuff is
cool.

Oh my gosh, Paul, only a city boy would
say that.

It's not like a crime, Emily, to be from
the city. You should come to Sioux
Falls. You might like it.

York is plenty big for me, Emily said.
She had lived in Nebraska her whole
life. She'd told Paul that, and he had not
forgotten. Flames lit up different parts of
her face.

JEFFREY ELLINGER

Once I've got my vet degree, she said,
I'm working on my dad's ranch and
never leaving. It's the only thing I've
ever wanted to do.

You don't want to visit other countries?

Why? Emily asked, so firmly that Paul
couldn't think of an answer. He only
hoped that, with time, he could show
her. They kept by the fire, and the
boyish-looking Paul learned that Emily
identified as a Christian but believed in
God as she believed in the stars above
their heads, the warmth coming from the
fire, the brown dirt at their feet; and so
he explained to Emily his belief that
those who don't accept Christ as their
savior are, sadly, doomed to hell.

You make it sound way too serious,
Paul. It's gentler than that. I think it is.

Emily was so pretty, Paul didn't argue.
Their theology discussion over, it was
time for her to drive back to her dad's
ranch. They gave each other a hug, one
Paul hasn't forgotten. Summer nearing
its end, the following week Emily would
go back to school. Her campus was an
hour away, but, as Paul saw it, she may
as well have been going to the moon.
To make sure she didn't travel with a

less-worthy astronaut, Paul planned to
divulge everything at her going-away
party. Lay all his feelings bare.

Disposable tablecloths covered the
picnic tables, piled with grilled meats
and macaroni salad and chips. Balloons,
weighted with small sacks of marbles,
wished her luck. Heavy coolers full of
pop. Hold on to your plates, the
headmaster announced, or watch them
fly across the field.

I'll be down at my dad's every weekend,
Emily said. A cup flew across the dusty
prairie. One of the boys ran after it.
You'll be around, won't you?

You betcha, Paul said. I'll be around. My
work here isn't done.

Good, Emily said. Maybe next time I see
you you'll be a proper cowboy. And she
gave Paul a playful punch on the arm.
The slug gave Paul a faint bruise that
would appear the next day, one whose
fading seemed more meaningful than
any other bruise he would ever earn.

Without any more ceremony Emily went
and stood by her father, a man with a
salt-and-pepper moustache, worn but
polished boots, a shirt both starched

and ironed. His jeans were faded but clean. His body had a used, strong quality but his eyes were youthful and alive: he was happy to have a daughter like Emily. Paul watched as the proud rancher put his arm around his daughter, enveloping her. Seeing the weathered man, Paul wondered what he could possibly say. How could he explain the things he planned to do? Marry Emily, then what? Take her on trips around the world? With what money? Have sex with her? In that moment the thought of even liking Emily seemed so absurd that Paul wanted to dig a hole and bury himself in it.

When the party came to an end and everyone had said their goodbyes and good lucks, Emily sat in the passenger seat of her father's heavy duty pickup—with two wheels on each of the rear axles—and Paul remembers this most of all, her special wave. There might still be a chance, he thought. In the next moment locked eyes with Emily's father, whose stare had such disdain it created a chalky taste in Paul's mouth that he could not produce a milliliter of saliva. Paul dropped his hand and the pickup started with a rumble. The heavy machine inched away, taking Emily down the bumpy gravel road. Less than a month later, sick with agony after receiving an email in which Emily told him to focus on Christ and not on her, Paul would leave as well. They would never see each other again.

—

Farther south, Paul planned. A friend said that Austin was the only place to be. You gotta get down here, man, the friend said. I'm telling you, if you move to Austin you're going to wonder why you didn't do it sooner.

Paul's friend in Texas owned a house just as Paul's old classmate Ryan Kaufman owned a house. But Ryan lived in a West River town in South Dakota, on land blatantly stolen from Natives. The idea of a friend owning property in prosperous Austin made Paul worry he did not have something real of his own. But he let it pass, and in that last week at the ranch he kept repeating to himself: First God, then relationships, then the places we go, that's the stuff that counts. Monthly mortgages and cumbersome bills forced the adults in his small hometown into a staid existence that Paul wanted to shirk, no matter the worldly cost. So after putting in his two weeks and telling himself the move to Texas had to be right, he prepared again. A couple kids at the ranch might've once cared about Paul's leaving, but those boys were long gone, making trouble in other parts of Nebraska. Before leaving, Paul did what he would do in the coming years whenever it came time to make a move. He packed while listening to the same song on repeat—"Love Song for a Savior" by Jars of Clay—and after he'd finished packing he kneeled beside the bed that he would soon leave behind and said one last prayer (or, in later years, repeated a purposeful blotting-out sort of meditation, leading into an admonishment that this is right), and at last he got dinner at his favorite place to eat, in this case a gas station close to the interstate. After that Paul drove south, without telling anyone in South Dakota. That way, no one could talk him out of it. Not until Paul got to Texas did he call. And while Dad sounded upset, what could be done? His son was grown.

Just poor decision making, Paul could hear echoing from hundreds of miles away. To drown out the discouraging voices he listened to an audiobook recommended by the friend in Austin, about a universe without God. Paul was not ready for a worldview as radical as that, but he respected his friend, an editor he'd met while interning at a Christian rock magazine outside Austin. Paul considered his friend to be one of the smarter individuals he had ever known, and some of the author's ideas on agnosticism did make some sense, he began to think as he listened: if it's a miracle that a Supreme Being created everything, then it must be equally miraculous, if not more so, to think that this is all random.

His first night in Austin Paul and his friend smoked weed—a first for Paul—and talked about the myth of creation and all that Paul would now be involved in, like barbeques and live music and art and women. And it struck Paul, in his altered state, that he had never had sex before, and having it, even clumsily, might be the cure to all of his problems. Paul tried to explain the epiphany to his editor friend, but the friend just laughed, which made Paul laugh, and also think, for a brief moment, that everything was perfect.

That first weekend they threw a house party, where Paul drank his first beers. Loud music played in the backyard, heavy with the gravity of good-looking women, more than Paul had ever seen in one place, and many with tattoos. A couple of girls Paul had known through the college radio station back in the Middle West had put ink in their bodies: one had a cross on her wrist, and another, who deejayed in the slot before him, had a literary quote tattooed on her forearm. Paul never read the novel, but as he looked around at the moving paintings in their short shorts and slinky tops, he wondered if he should start getting into esoteric fiction. Everyone in Austin seemed so full of art. He stepped over the crunchy brown grass, nodding at the educated beauties like the naive farm boy he was. Fit then, Paul wore shorts—not the long cargos of his past—and a form-fitting t-shirt that read, *Fishin' with South Dakota FHA-Hero*. The white fish against a blue background contrasted with his tanned skin and sun-washed hair. Paul took a long drink and approached one of the partygoers. They had locked eyes and did so again.

If he'd come up with a more original beginning, Phoebe Black might've been the one to transform Paul into something he would never be, an urbane literature professor with friends who worked for universities and received grants. As it is, Nice tattoo are the first two words Paul Bethel ever said to Phoebe Black, and it's like they would never recover from them. Paul would try to overcome, and in her weaker moments Phoebe would concede to her best friends that there was hope for, as she would say, That one guy who comes over sometimes.

In the backyard at the party Phoebe gave Paul a bemused smile. She'd heard pick-up lines about her tattoos, enough she wondered if maybe she'd made a mistake in getting them. Yes, Phoebe Black of Austin---like Phoebe Blacks in Portland and Madison and Asheville---wanted attention, just not that much attention. But there it was in front of her, in the form of a grinning man who looked as fresh off the wagon as they could come. She liked his sunglasses, though. He must take care of things, she thought.

I'm Paul, he said, extending his hand with straightforward vigor.

Phoebe, she said, and they touched for the first time.

Good to meet you, Paul said. His shoulders relaxed. Cool angel, he said, pointing to her upper arm, and almost, but not quite, touched her again.

JEFFREY ELLINGER

Oh my God, I got that one a long time ago.

The colors are alive, Paul said. Being bold enlivened him, and he thought, since he was already behind, he may as well ask: Are you a believer?

In God? Jesus, no . . . I mean, are you?

Since asking Jesus into his heart in a dorm room in Brookings, Paul had been certain he would answer such a question with a clear and sure yes. It was one thing mitigating his parents' worry; at least they knew where their son would go when he died. But faced with this almond-haired girl, her form pneumatic in a white tank top, her thighs bulging from shorts, Paul found himself considering how to answer the question of the existence of God.

I am, he said. But it's not like the way crazy people believe. It's a personal relationship, you know?

Personal relationship, Phoebe said. She took a drink from her beer. Condensation made the glass wet, and as the bottle released from her mouth there was a popping sound. Sounds serious, man.

But Phoebe's attractiveness made Paul think quicker, not slower. I mean, he said, not that serious. I'm actually interested in all kinds of religions. Aren't you?

—

And not like all that Hollywood bullshit, Phoebe was saying. They had found lawn chairs and she sat across from him. Their legs interlocked like the teeth of a zipper. I'm interested in the historical Buddhism. Not the trendy shit.

Paul shook his head in agreement with as much positivity as he could muster without betraying everything about himself. The sun went down. The party thinned, and they got each other's numbers on the best night of Paul Bethel's life—he might even still say that—and as he slept alone in his new basement bedroom Paul did not pray for forgiveness for having a buzz, not like he thought he would. He only prayed he could get to know Phoebe Black.

Back then, Paul would have never hypothesized a bleak future for himself, would never have thought the only time in his life when he would consider a prayer answered would be the one he said that night, but it was answered all the same. Several evenings a week they went to shows, often at Emo's, and while Phoebe's reasoning for going out with Paul would always be vague, choosing someone like Paul didn't need much explaining. At that age and in that town one did not need a man to have skills and accomplishments, or even a car. He only needed to be willing to hang out. Also, Phoebe liked Paul's build and genuineness. He was good-looking in an odd way, though he wasn't as tall as she would've liked, since she was five feet nine niches and he wasn't a speck more than six feet. It helped that she was young, just twenty-one, and needed someone to the support the pursuit of going out. He could be that support, with help from a job found through a temp agency at a company that sold generic drugs. It wasn't what Paul wanted to do with his life, but the drudgery bought drinks and tickets, filled up the gas tank when Phoebe wanted to go to Schlitterbahn, and Barton Springs too, when she could find no one else to go.

Their routine lasted for most of a year, and more than once Paul believed they'd be together forever. He'd stay overnight in her messy room in her shared house and tell stories about how he used to believe sex was supposed to wait until marriage, and she would laugh and ask, So you didn't want a girl doing this? Then she'd proceed to do something he had always dreamed of someone doing that would make him wonder what he could have been thinking, waiting so long. But those times were always broken by Paul's pressing her, wanting to become something more than, as he complained, just sleepover and show buddies. So their relationship came to an abrupt end, one Paul could've seen coming, if he could've ever seen anything. It started when he hinted at her coming back with him to South Dakota for the Christmas holidays. Sincerely, Paul thought, he could engender a softness in Phoebe if she saw his bucolic upbringing, stir in her a certain brand of loyalty. He asked after he'd already invited her to other family events, like Easter and Thanksgiving. He'd tried all the tactics: the diffident plea, the humble petition, though never the ultimatum. Paul had always been afraid of what would come from such a thing. But what good was it knowing someone that pretty if nobody ever got to see her with him? He went with the ultimatum, though not in person, knowing how hard that would be. Paul sent an email, and almost as soon as he had, Phoebe sent a reply.

> Paul,
>
> I'm previously engaged that weekend, and since I never seem to go on these trips, I know it wouldn't have worked anyway. Don't you think it's time we stopped this? You're nice, but I think we should find separate paths for our lives. Bye now.
>
> Love,
> Phoebe

Not as hard as Paul thought it'd be, to see Phoebe go. She'd been, he told anyone who asked, immature, if you want to put a label on it. And while one could easily see that Paul didn't believe what he said, it did seem like he got along well enough. But without Phoebe, nothing was left in Austin. Paul's friend appeared ready to live on his own again, and Paul hated his temp job more than any job he had ever had, which was a decent statement considering he started working at the age of thirteen as a corn detasseler. Without a distinct idea of what he wanted to be, the conclusion was *I can live anywhere*. The only thing

Paul knew for sure was that he wanted
to visit Europe, especially Barcelona
and Paris. And he wanted to do it right.
He didn't want to be a backpacked brute
scorching his way through the peaks of
civilization. He had just enough funds for
a short trip, but where? He had no
desire other than Europe. Other places
existed but were not the right kind of
places for someone like Paul, who
needed, in a pinch, the tastes and
sounds of somewhere like home,
someone to speak to him in words he
halfway understood, maybe give him a
grilled hamburger with, if they had it,
Mrs. Dash. So he regrouped and came
up with an idea he thought brilliant, even
if no one else did. California. In
childhood, watching commercials for
bubble gum or skateboards, California
seemed like a place colored in pastels
and neon, a place where people wore
white high-tops in a cool way. As a
grown man Paul had a hunch the state
would be different than what he
imagined in youth, but he was ready.
Austin prepared him. No friends waited
in Los Angeles. Paul had only steam
from years of staying close to home,
and he used that energy to power his
way west along the desert highways, his
car's wheels propelling him to the
precipice of something big. Never
before, as Paul saw in the rearview

mirror, had he looked better. Phoebe
had sometimes even acted jealous after
a party, saying things like, You didn't
think she was as pretty as me, do you?
And there'd been other times, outside of
bars, when strangers had come up to
Paul and said he was cute, like the
cheerleader who kissed him in high
school. As Paul drove westward he
thumbed through those memories, along
with a conversation with Dad on his last
day in Austin: Your mother and I know
you have potential, Dad said. We don't
want you to waste it.

After they'd hung up Paul imagined his
parents talking about what could be
done, if anything, or if maybe their son
was lost for good. With a unilateral belief
to the contrary, Paul sensed himself
going in the right direction. The road
west, clear and dry, acted as an
expression of freedom and intoxicated
Paul so that he did not complain that no
one sat in his passenger seat, snoring
lightly after a big lunch, squeezing his
hand when the weather got bad, or—
though he'd seen and heard of couples
arguing over such things—asking, Are
you sure we're taking the right road?
Loud ska music played. The scenery of
the dry land. Paul forgot about any
ghost of a better life alongside him.
Breaking down would be for someone

else, on some other trip. For only so long.

The first signs of deterioration came at the edge of Texas, and when Paul first noticed he didn't bother stopping at a gas station. Paul could easily get hoodwinked, as he knew so little about cars. And the mechanic could never be as honest as Harold, Dad's mechanic back home. Not knowing a thing aside from where the gas went—and even that Paul didn't learn until he got his own car in his early twenties—Paul kept going. He did not want to cause alarm by calling home. Somewhere past Flagstaff Paul knew something was wrong, and he considered stopping, but he did not want to. He put blinders on and accelerated on the highway, wavy from the heat, and instead of an immediate propulsion from the engine to the pistons there was a pause, then an awful lurch, violent enough that it made Paul's face flush. Then the car regained its power, and once up to speed Paul put it in cruise control, and for a few moments everything seemed okay. The air conditioning went full blast on his face and Paul would've appeared, to a car passing, to be in a groove, tapping his hand on the steering wheel while singing along to Five Iron Frenzy's newest album. He thought about how strange life might be in California, but maybe that's how it is for everyone moving to the West Coast from the Middle West. After passing a semi Paul pressed the gas pedal again. Nothing. Again he pressed. Nothing.

No, Paul said, stomping on the gas. No. No. No.

Quickly enough he thought to put his hazards on and pull over—two drivers sped by, one of them honking and the other staring—and once he'd rolled to a stop Paul's thoughts went back to home. He had never been the guy on the side of the road. Dad took every car in the Bethel family for oil changes, often a good thousand miles short of the recommended changing time, and he did other things too, things Paul would've never had the money for, like new tires and brakes and springs. Paul's car always ran smoothly, as he remembered Dad's cars running smoothly. Never had anyone in the family been on the side of the road waving at fumes, pouring liquids in the hood, channeling underneath the vehicle looking for a mystical issue. A flip phone on the passenger seat. Paul looked at the device for a good minute before he picked it up and called his brother-in-law in Yankton. Jim answered right away, as he always did, and Paul was happier than usual for that.

Jimmy Jim, Paul said.

Dizzy Paul, what's up there? How's the trip?

Good good, but hey, Jim. Not to be too of-the-ordinary here, but do you have any experience with breaking down? I mean, your car. I think I might have a situation like that now.

Jim had to laugh. Paul would present a serious topic like being stranded so nonchalantly. Still, Jim asked, because he cared, Crappers, Paul, you all right?

I am. Just don't know what's wrong with my car. It was accelerating weird, like it would go forward after I gave it gas, but there's this pause. And now it's just stopped altogether.

Boy, if I was there I might know for sure, Paul, but that sounds like a transmission issue.

Paul had hoped Jim would have better news. As soon as he'd started dating Joanne, Paul's sister, years before, Jim

had infused good humor into the Bethel
family. Carefree, Jim bought things
Paul's father would've never allowed,
like a used Ford Mustang, new Jordans,
and clothes from Abercrombie and
Fitch.

You think I could get going again? Paul
asked. In the distance he saw the
outline of striated canyons, colored
purple and red before sundown. I mean,
is there anything I can do?

Not sure if you can, Paul. Have you
called your dad?

Not yet. I was thinking of doing that
once I got in town. You think you could
find me a number for roadside
assistance? I mean, I wonder who I
should be calling now, a tow truck?

I'll find one. Hold on a sec. So Jim did
just that and before they hung up Paul
promised he'd call home as soon as he
got into town. After Jim wished him good
luck, Paul was alone again. Waiting for
the tow, thoughts of money flooded his
mind. The idea that cars would always
last was a warped one he'd inherited
from his dad, who extended the life of all
his vehicles. In some pathetic corner of
his mind Paul had been hoping to buy a

new car once he got to L.A., but in the
passenger seat of a tow truck that stunk
of wintergreen chewing tobacco he
knew that plan would have to be
adjusted. The tow-truck driver dropped
Paul and his car off at a garage. Paul
then walked a mile to the nearest hotel
and in his room sat on a hard bed with a
smooth comforter. Mom and Dad would
be sleeping, he knew, but they'd answer
right away. Paul pictured where they
kept their phone, close to the bed. He
could see it ring before Mom answered.

Pauly, my son, she said, all woozy, like
from a dream. Then, more alert, she
asked, You're done driving for the day?
What time is it?

A little past midnight, sorry to call so
late. Just wanted to tell you guys I made
it safe and got a hotel room. Thought
you'd want to know.

That's nice, Pauly. That's very good.
How was your drive?

Hello? Dad said from another phone. It
was a conference call now.

Dad, hey, you're awake too?

JEFFREY ELLINGER

Yeah, Dad said. What's going on, Bud?
You make it to the next big city?

I'm down for the night, that's for sure.

Where are you? Mom asked.

Super 8 in Kingman, Arizona. Could use
some softer pillows, but it's not too bad.

We're glad you made it, Mom said,
sounding like she was going back to
sleep.

Right, okay, but also I should tell you
guys before I go that I had a little car
trouble. Then Paul quickly added, But
don't worry about it. I can get it figured
out.

Car trouble, Dad said, with an edge to
his awakened voice. What do you mean
car trouble?

That's kind of what it is, Dad. Something
with the transmission, Jim thinks.

Transmission, Dad said. Oh Judas, how
did you make it into town?

I got a tow.

Oh Pauly, Mom said.

But it's not that big of a deal, Paul
assured them, in a way that could not
have assured them at all.

How much was the tow? Dad asked.

Like a hundred bucks, Paul said, though
it was twice that. They took it to this
shop and the guy said they do good
work, so I could be up and running by
tomorrow.

You won't be running again in a day,
Dad said. Not with transmission
problems. It'll take longer than that.

It looked like the kind of place that does
good work, Dad. It did not, but Paul
couldn't say that.

It takes time to fix a transmission, Dad
said. Where are you going to stay?

Here, I guess, but listen, guys, I don't
want you to be riled up. I just wanted to
let you know what's happening. It's
nothing to worry about.

Paul, Mom said. Don't be like that. We
can worry about you.

JEFFREY ELLINGER

Sorry, I'm just saying, don't worry, he
said, repeating himself. How about I call
you in the morning and give you an
update? I'm pretty tired now.

By the time Paul woke up he had three
missed calls and two new voicemails.
One from Dad, asking, specifically, what
the mechanic had said, and the other
from Mom, saying, We have a plan.
Paul knew what it'd be. They'd come
down with a car, the one Dad used for
trips to sell insurance, and his parents
would wait as Paul's got fixed so Paul
could move along with the working one.
We're looking for a new color anyway,
Mom said, and Paul didn't argue. It was
his best and only option. In the
meantime he visited the repair shop, a
place for things grown men knew, where
he sensed the proprietors saw him as
someone who did not belong.

Transmission's shot, the mechanic said.
He wrenched on the underbelly of
another car lifted on a hoist. The name
on the oval patch said Steve.

So I need a new one? Paul asked.

Yep, Steve said.

And you guys do that? I know it's not like a gas filter, but can you get a new one?

We can, Steve said as he cranked into his work. But I wouldn't recommend it. He stopped and looked at the tool as if it should be another. Paul followed him to a toolbox. Let me show you, Steve said, shutting a drawer. The sound of clanking metal, and Paul followed him again, to a grimy corner of the garage, where they kept an old register with raised metal buttons and receipt paper in a spool. Steve started to punch up the numbers. By the time he finished the cost was remarkably close to what Dad had predicted.

I see, Paul said. That's the total then? He pointed to the four-figure number.

Yep, Steve said. Wouldn't replace a transmission on a vehicle like this.

Sure, Paul said. Sure. Well, I appreciate all this. Let me think about it, if I could. Would I be able to leave it now? I'm heading to California, so I'll make some arrangements and be back.

Yep, fine, Steve said as he walked away, leaving the projected numbers

beside pink carbon copies of bills
hanging on a rack.

There was nothing else to do. Exiting
the garage into the oppressive heat,
Paul knew one thing: how he would feel
when his parents arrived, indebted. In
the hotel that night he dreamed he
became a baby. Day after next Mom
and Dad arrived. They ate at a sit-down
restaurant on the outskirts of town.

Paul, Dad said, putting the keys to their
car on the table. You're free to use this.
It's yours. But your mother and I were
talking on the way down here and we
think it might be a good idea if you came
home. We don't think it's a good idea to
move somewhere just to get away from
someone or something.

His upfront tone caught his son off-
guard. But Paul couldn't stop now. He
might revert to the womb. I'm not
running away, guys, he said. Really, I'm
not.

We still think it'd be a good idea to come
home, Mom said. Do you have a job out
there?

Paul stuffed more food in his gape. He
could remember the depression of

college, when he could hardly eat, and he knew how much that had troubled his parents. Now, as he wolfed down sausage and pancakes and eggs, all in big bites, then wetted them with thick brown syrup and big gulps of orange juice and pop, he hoped he looked like the happiest son in America.

I've been looking, Paul said, the words tumbling out. But I'm telling you, it's going to be a lot easier than at home. I know you guys think it's perfect in South Dakota, but it doesn't work for everybody. It doesn't work for me.

Mom and Dad did not reply, and that, for Paul, was a feat. It seemed to him that their silence arose from appreciation at his outburst of honesty. That must have been what made them mute, Paul was sure. Another moment passed and Mom took a look at her husband, who said what Paul would later repeat, sometimes even out loud to himself, whenever he got the urge to go back home.

Life's about choices, Dad said. And while Paul understood what that meant, that this choice of his was all wrong, the boy had too much respect for his father to say anything in return. Paul just

49

shook his head in agreement as he
continued to eat as much, and as fast,
as he could.

—

Leaving his parents at the hotel
conjured a terse goodbye. Dad simply
shook Paul's hand, and they had a brief
period where they all thought Mom
might cry, but she didn't, and so all that
was left to do was for Paul to say thank
you once more, hug them each again—
straight on for his mom and from the
side for his dad—and go to his new
used car. Paul honked as he drove
away in the baby-blue sedan, a silver
ichthus screwed into the body. He
wanted to allay any concerns that he
might be leaving in bad spirits, but the
religious fish made him self-conscious.
Whatever faith he had left Paul wanted
kept a secret.

Getting to the next stop didn't help
matters. Paul had never seen a woman
nude, other than Phoebe every other
month or so for a year, and there would
be many to admire inside the hedonistic
dens along the long strip of asphalt,
rolled out like a red carpet. Paul found
the cheapest hotel he could, away from
the main drag, as Dad might've said.
The sun setting, Paul went out and

brushed past packs of men and women his age striding by in drunken hopefulness. In the casinos elderly folks pulled handles of slot machines, looking as if they had come to Vegas to wither in the dry heat that blew over Paul as he left one air-conditioned castle for another. After eating supper alone, Paul paced on the sidewalk across the street from a strip club, and when he was sure he wouldn't burst into flames he crossed the street at a brisk pace—almost too brisk. Paul didn't notice the silver Lexus running a red light. A loud breeze whooshed by, then the blast of a horn, but as Paul started walking again he could only be thankful.

Motherfucker almost ran you over, bro, the bouncer said at the door. Come on in. No charge.

A better turn of events Paul could not have imagined. While eating alone, every possible interaction with the man at the door had gone through his mind. An unspoken handshake? What if he said something like, You sure you're ready for this, buddy? What if he just laughed? The near-death experience alleviated all that and Paul went in, glad that he'd been nearly run over on the most famous road in America.

JEFFREY ELLINGER

Inside the darkened place, illuminated by neon strips of light, it came as a surprise to Paul to smell Sunday smorgasbord after church. Loud hair metal pulsed through his body as he ordered a gin and tonic, the only drink he knew, and he followed that one with two more. Sturdy gold poles sprouted out of the black stage, looking as if they supported the very structure of the building. The woman dancing wore no top and a string. She gyrated expertly on the steel. Phoebe had been Paul's only, though she had been just as utilitarian as Paul when it came to love. The alcohol loosened Paul and the women began to seem approachable, even though he knew he stuck out among the flashy businessmen and the boys who looked like they might be on spring break and the ghostly others at the end of the bar. Paul got another drink and decided to stay as long as it lasted, remembering a true love. They'd never spoken beyond a hello, but whenever Paul saw her at the college radio station, or passed her smoking cigarettes outside the student union, he would wonder who she liked more: the Beatles, or Belle and Sebastian. A confidence surrounded her, like someone who didn't worry about whether she would ever get married.

She put buttons and patches on her bag, which she did not wear on her back like every other student at State but across her chest, like a professor. For almost the last three years she had been Paul's dream, even after he became a zealous believer who could no longer entertain ideas of sex before marriage.

Paul did a double-take. A woman dancing nearby looked so much like his fantasy. He watched her dance near a large black man with gold rings on his fingers, and whenever she writhed in his direction Paul turned his eyes away, like he hadn't been looking. Then she was very near, giving him the kind of smile she must have used before, the smile she must have known reminded men of a special girl who didn't belong in a place like this.

Want a dance? she asked.

Please, Paul said. I mean, if that's not a problem.

That's why I'm here, babe. And she took Paul's hand and led him away to a private area, where she grasped his inner thighs.

JEFFREY ELLINGER

Are you from here? Paul asked as she
eased her backside down onto his lap.

I'm from here now, baby, she said, and
pushed into his stiffness. And I want you
to be happy.

Right, it's that you just look so much like
this girl I knew. I . . .

With a patient kindness the dancer
turned and put her hands on Paul's
shoulders. Just sit back and relax,
honey, she said. So he did, settling into
the type of comfort that comes from
being near someone after years of
isolation. After she finished her time she
went to another room, guarded by a
mountain of a man—his arms covered in
tribal tattoos and looking like he could
drink protein shakes like water---while
Paul uncomfortably walked to the front
entrance and out into the desert. In bed
at the hotel that night her smell
remained so Paul masturbated to the
thought of her, and in the coldness after
he found it surprising that he did not
want to die. The next morning he left a
tip on the dresser, went out to his
parents' car, and drove the rest of the
way to Los Angeles.

—

Work didn't take long to find in California. Paul liked the job, delivering machined parts, and believed he could do it for a long time, moving things from place to place. People needed what he had and were happy to see him most of the time. No longer did he have to look over his shoulder for micromanagers, like at the temp job packaging generic drugs in Austin, and there were no teenage boys to redirect, like at the ranch in Nebraska. Those kinds of jobs he wanted to be forever rid of, and by driving on the interminable interstates, he could be. The traffic didn't even bother him. Paul would put in a mix CD and look out the window and be amazed that he lived in Los Angeles, of all places. He had made a way for himself. All he needed was love. In pursuit of that need, Paul found a nondenominational church with small-group meetings where they drank beer and talked about faith, but more about how their faith related to dating. Going to a church like that, Paul thought, could be a good way to meet someone who had taken the same winding road. Considering Paul's fading faith, he knew he would never contribute to the

services, but he also wanted to meet
The One, and he wouldn't meet her in
his apartment. It had running water and
a roof but not the amenities men his age
were beginning to have, like wood floors
and high ceilings and recessed lighting.
Meeting her by going to rock shows and
volunteering at soup kitchens seemed
forced to Paul, and he couldn't meet her
on a campus, as he had no plans of
going to graduate school. Church would
have to suffice, and one Sunday
morning the pastor—who wore a
hooded sweatshirt and black jeans and
sported a scraggly soul patch, with small
black plugs in both his earlobes—read
from Acts. After the reading he asked
the congregation to pair up into thought
pockets, as he called them, to discuss
the passage projected on the screen
behind him.

And when you break it down, the pastor
said as the congregation rustled,
searching for their partners, break it
down like you were one of the dudes
back then living in the first century and
your biggest worries were keeping your
one donkey alive and making enough
bread for your family so they don't
starve, all right?

Forced laughter filled the cavernous space as Paul turned, and from a corner of his eye he received an endearing smile one could only hope to see when turning to a stranger. So pretty and naïve, she had crooked teeth. Paul couldn't help but have thoughts of what it'd be like to move to the country and start a farm with her. They would drink the milk from their cows and in the evenings eat hearty meat and wash it down with the wine from their grapes, then off to bed for a night of lovemaking, after which they'd discuss their once prehistoric thinking but also be united in their knowledge that there is a God for them, somewhere, though not like it used to be. Not like it used to be, Paul repeated in his head as he heard her talk about what they were supposed to be talking about, but just as soon Paul's thoughts drifted back to the dream, and he'd take her in his arms and once again she'd come to rapture, then hold her in steady bliss till the morning came, oh till the morning.

Her name was Jamie, and while Paul had never seen her there at church before, he had purposely sat near her in the back with these discussions in mind. She wore a skirt with tights underneath. A blouse with a bird stitched onto it. They discussed the scenario for almost ten minutes, as the pastor instructed, while Paul imagined his future with her on an idyllic farm.

You think so? Jamie was countering again. She had challenged Paul on every point, centered around the premise that our modern times are too complicated and thus harder than the life of people in the Iron Age. I'd say the opposite, Jamie said. We have it way too easy. Everything is so taken care of now. Like with the nonprofit group I help run in Nigeria. When I go over there I get the feeling of living in a time like Jesus's time, a time when things were so much more basic, and I think awful. Don't you think?

That's true, Paul said, lying. So true. He wanted to keep Jamie smiling her crooked smile. Later, when the final praise and worship came to a denouement and the live rock music began to play, Paul seized the moment and asked, So what are you up to tonight, Jamie? Any big plans?

God, she said, which Paul thought was a sophisticated thing for her to say. I've just been going all week. I'll probably go home and read the *Times* and play guitar. That sounds amazing right now. What're you up to?

A bike ride, I think. Do you ride? It's not very popular here, I know.

I love that, Paul. I love bikes so much. You go a lot?

Definitely. All the time. Always in forward motion, that's kinda my motto.

Sounds like a good motto, Paul. Paul, I didn't get your last name.

Paul Bethel, and you know, Jamie . . . He paused.

Clayton, she reciprocated, and smiled her smile again.

You know, Jamie Clayton, if you ever wanted to go bike riding, we could do that.

Oh my God, Paul, I'd love that. Let me give you my email address. And though it wasn't her number, Paul was content to have something to go by, to put in his pocket and think about, the way she curved her letters on one of the church's let us get to know you cards, how she

put a smiley face at the end. He emailed
her that night.

Paul, hey, Jamie replied the next day.
It's so nice to hear from you. I'm happy
you still want to go biking. Sadly, I am
so dreadfully busy this week again, but I
think I would have time on Thursday
night, if you do. I'm free any time after
7pm. Please tell me if this works for you.
So glad to hear you're having a good
day. Bye now.

Paul would be free Thursday. He would
move heaven and earth to be free
Thursday, and so they met at a park
between their two apartments. The first
thing Paul learned, a thing that only
helped cement the fact that he would
someday marry Jamie Clayton, was that
she didn't want to move back to
Wisconsin. There was nothing for her
there.

My sister lives in Florida, she said as
they rode. Jamie wore black biking
shorts, shorter and more form-fitting
than Paul could've ever imagined. My
mom and my stepdad live in Texas. But
my dad and my stepmom live in New
York City.

I don't ever want to live in South Dakota again, Paul said. I love my family, don't get me wrong, but I can't go back to a place where the biggest goal in life is to get married and have kids. I mean, no offense. Is your sister married? Sorry if I'm asking boring questions. Paul finished with a sour smile that he wished were more confident, but it was all he had.

Hey, that's okay, Paul. I mean, no, she's not married. She's lived with the same guy for about five years. Do you want to get married?

Married? Paul chuckled, then lied again. No, I don't need to get married to be happy. I just think it's interesting to hear about other people and why and when they did it. I just want to live, you know?

Me too, Jamie said, and Paul knew by some deep sense waiting types have— like the kind Barthes writes of—that he would have to sell himself, like a set of knives or a vacuum, for Jamie to fall for him. He had no six-pack of abs or European-built wagon to take on weekend trips to Joshua Tree.

They stopped to eat at a vegan restaurant. Then they went to a bar nearby and drank beers on the porch, enjoying the eerily predictable weather. She smiled more than she gave a neutral look, Paul thought. The admiration she voiced for how he biked—sitting upright and coasting while she pedaled hard—seemed to be an admission of something. But after he paid and they left together Paul couldn't help but be yanked back by a nagging voice saying everything has been preordained. You can do nothing to change your station. All heartbreak is yours to bear.

So, this was fun, Jamie said on the sidewalk at a quiet corner. Her bike rested against her hip as she put on her helmet. Thank you so much for the meal and the beer, everything.

No problem, Paul said. I hope you had a good time.

I did, Jamie said. It was time for a kiss now, or a hug, or even a playful tap on the shoulder. But nothing seemed right to Paul, and as the moments slipped by Jamie began to wheel her bike away. Maybe I'll see you again, she said, partway down the block. At church?

Yeah, see you there, Paul shouted, but Jamie was far enough away that he wasn't sure she heard. He turned his attention to the white carton in his hand. Jamie had said several times to take the leftovers, but as Paul walked down the street alongside parked cars—bike gears ticking—he knew wouldn't save them, even though she said they'd taste better than the hot meal. Save this and eat as a remembrance, she was saying, these last morsels. A block more and he had mounted his bike. He rode straight for a trash can, where he threw the carton away. Tonight cannot be all there is, he thought, unready to acquiesce to the leftovers being their last communion.

That evening Paul sent an email, recycling most of the events of the evening and telling Jamie that he had eaten the leftovers. He wrote, They were just as good as you said they'd be. At the end he slipped in his main reason for writing: What I really wanted to ask is if you'd be interested in going to the drive-in that's pretty close to my place. They're playing *Princess Bride*! Paul wrapped up the message with a cocksure *Your friend*, which belied how much he rued not embracing her at their parting. He hadn't even asked for a second date. A man is supposed to do that, he thought, getting ready for work

the next morning: always be closing.
The email, he hoped, would realign her
perception of him as a candid individual,
and, more importantly, a man. He even
asked for her phone number in a
postscript he believed to be suave. In
the coming days, as Paul drove around
the city for work, he went through the
best-case scenarios. Her response
would say Sorry for being a bit
standoffish, but I think you're handsome.
Then a wink, and at the end would be
the prize, her phone number. For three
days Paul waited, and on each he laid
out all the possibilities before him. Then
came the response.

> Hey Paul,
>
> Just wanted to say thanks for the
> great time on Thursday. The bike
> ride and beer and everything. It
> was so nice to meet you.
> Unfortunately, I didn't really feel
> a spark. I hope you understand.
> Best of luck.
>
> Best,
> Jamie

The word spark punctured Paul, and as
he drove around delivering each
package he preached to himself that

you can't base a person's worth on one meeting. But no matter how much he orated to his broken heart, none of it rang true, and he had to admit he hadn't swept her off her feet like the dating books said to do. Be wild at heart, kiss dating goodbye, sing the blues like jazz. To avoid the shame, Paul never went back to that church, and in the months that followed he began to think maybe he not only didn't have the spark for Jamie, but for anyone in L.A. Everyone in that sunny pocket of bubbled existence, he began to see, lived artificially after moving there from Ohio or Michigan. If lucky, they ended up as extras in bad summer blockbusters or in bit roles on sitcoms or already forgotten dramas. When that failed they moved to careers in restaurants and fitness clubs but stubbornly kept their conceited attitude. No, this wouldn't be the place for Paul Bethel. Time to move again, he resolved.

—

To Minneapolis, into one of the spare bedrooms in a house in the suburbs belonging to a college friend, unmarried but well off. Also no longer a Christian, Mike Morris owned a burgeoning tech company, and in the two years Paul

JEFFREY ELLINGER

would live with Mike they'd never be
friends, not like they once were. Their
rift arose, Paul believed, from Mike
never trusting Paul enough to work at
his company. Paul knew that if he could
just get a job there, real money would
start to come in, and he could be
important and no longer fall for anyone
who showed him attention. Instead of
planting a money tree in Mike's
backyard and going to happy hours with
those who might have looked like
Phoebe—now, in the Upper Midwest,
wearing coats and scarves instead of
shorts and sunglasses—Paul found a
job at a package delivery company and
began online dating, meeting women
who reminded him of shortcomings, not
theirs but his own.

After nearly two years and becoming
more disappointed with everything, Paul
left for Chicago. The package delivery
company gave him a transfer and Paul
moved in with another old friend, Tyler
Novena, who was becoming a doctor.
Living above Tyler and Tyler's college-
aged girlfriend in their unoccupied
upstairs, Paul realized how unhappy
he'd become, and that no matter how
many times he moved, things would
always be unsettled. Paul didn't voice
that fatal concern. He just lived on
Tyler's top floor and considered himself

lucky to have the arrangement. The low rent allowed Paul to enjoy exploring the city, the first place he'd lived that he considered a real city. L.A. had been too disparate and spread out. Austin was too small and laid-back, while Minneapolis was a grown-up Sioux Falls, with everyone hanging out in the same social circles as in high school. In Chicago one could sink their teeth, so he did. Paul even found a girlfriend. In her early thirties and working as a librarian, Jan Baker would be the last partner Paul could ever look back on with nothing but happiness, until the end, which he could only think of with bitterness. Paul never brought Jan home to his parents, who didn't call as much by then, nor did they ask which church he attended or what kind of big news he could share. They seemed to have come to terms with the fact that their only son would be a balding man who drove a truck and might go to hell when he died. That knowledge seemed to age them, and Paul avoided going home in their final years.

Then one day Paul came back to their apartment in Chicago to a man's grunts and Jan yelping louder than he had ever heard before. So Jan and Paul split the few things they shared in the meager Portage Park apartment. Leaving again for somewhere else didn't break Paul like he thought it might. He'd begun to think of words like "cheating" and "infidelity" as outdated puritanical concepts. Still, the whole dramatic ordeal did prompt another move, out of the small one-bedroom apartment he and Jan shared to an even smaller studio apartment in Seattle, and there in the gray city Paul didn't have any friends. He had chosen Seattle because he'd always been fascinated with the Pacific Northwest. As a deejay in college, playing bands like NoQo and Four Wood Madness, Paul had dreamed of moving west in the hopes of working at Hammer and Mouth Records, the most forward-thinking Christian music label, he believed. When Paul finally did get there, almost exactly ten years after sending Hammer and Mouth an earnest letter as a freshman at State—inquiring as to whether he could get a job—he drove to their headquarters in Magnolia and found they'd moved to Nashville. He imagined their new offices as nondescript alongside other businesses, not like the digs featured in the yearly VHS tapes sent out as promotion in the early aughts, workers skateboarding through the office showing off tattoos going by posters on the walls of bands like Danielson Famile and ironic ones of

Amy Grant. The unoccupied building represented something, and while Paul recognized it that first day in Seattle, he didn't wrestle with the uneasiness, knowing that to do so would unearth emotions he wanted to keep buried. He went back to work driving a big brown truck, delivering goods up and down the steep streets, and a part of Paul enjoyed the work, but moving to Seattle did cause him to lose his seniority within the company. He had to start from the bottom and work as a cover driver. They gave him the worst routes possible, with the heaviest, most back-breaking packages, and on the days Paul finished his route on time, management would force him to go back and help other drivers. In the rain Paul would grind his teeth and think if only Mike had given him a job at his company, if only Jan, if only Phoebe, if only Jamie, if only Emily, if only any of the others whose names have been lost to some illusory romantic ether had seen in him what he saw. Those hypotheticals haunted Paul, and he began to consider moving to New York and becoming a writer. He went over ideas for novels in his studio each night but was usually too exhausted to write and would forget almost as soon as he cracked his second beer. Sometimes, Paul still prayed, but the words always seemed forced, even in his own head, and no real communion occurred before passing out.

Only once did Mom and Dad come to Seattle to visit, and Paul had become so depressed he almost thought it a reasonable option when Dad jokingly asked, Maybe you want to come back to South Dakota and be a cowman? Paul tried to laugh it off, as if to say *I love my life and everything about it*, but after they left later that night he honestly considered the question. In that time Portland was coming up often in the media as a good place to live as a younger person, and Paul was still youngish. A decent amount of hair on his head. Maybe, he imagined, he could be one of those bearded men who drives a truck and says he's an artist so he can date a girl who wants to be with one but is still too naive to know which ones are the real artists. Paul, at the time, was starting to contribute to the contributor-fueled weblog *Feeling Magazine*, along with the paragon of progressive culture, *Sin*. He was receiving promising rejections from literary journals too. But, and there was always a but for Paul, he hadn't gone to Europe, and he wanted to be able to tell the ones he met about his trip through the most beautiful places on earth. A continent clouded Paul's daydreams in

Portland, where he had moved and worked as a delivery driver. He ate his lunch at a pizza place he often visited. A waitress brought him his order. Paul brushed debris from his work pants and grinned at the pie, loaded with meat and cheese.

That guy took your spot, the waitress said as she set down the pizza. She glanced at a non-regular in another booth.

I saw that, Paul said, a slice already on his plate. There had been no love interests in Portland. No prospects either. He blinked and a year went by. What was he thinking? He asked, Did you take my plaque down?

Flour dusted her apron. Her hair messy, the waitress had an unconventional face with a big sexual nose that fascinated Paul. She patted him on the hand. I'll get to work on getting a new plaque back there, a gold one. We wouldn't want to lose our best customer.

I'm Paul, by the way, he said. He cleaned his hands with a napkin, then reached out. They shook hands.

Nice to meet you, Paul. I'm Elise.

JEFFREY ELLINGER

Good to meet you. I come in here all the
time. I was thinking we'd never meet.

Well, glad you said something. And she
began to walk away, but before going
too far she turned, smiling as she asked,
I'll see you around?

For sure, he said, and Paul couldn't help
it: he watched her backside. It seemed
to him to have the kind of shape that
would inspire a group text among
jealous girlfriends, asking each other if
that thing is even real.

The check arrived with a phone number
written on it, but Paul left a normal tip,
thinking any other approach could be
characterized as problematic. After that,
it didn't take long. Only three months in
Paul recognized Elise as The One in
many ways. She was attentive and
adoring, and Paul got to the point early
on where he told her of his deepest
insecurities: losing his hair, his lack of a
great job, the paucity of his
accomplishments. He didn't know why
he wanted to unload so badly, but he did
it anyway, almost every night for the first
two weeks of their living together. Elise
reminded him of his own mom when
she'd say: Everything isn't as bad as

you make it out to be. Or when she'd use reason against his scattered worries: You can just check that worry off your list.

One night at the end of their beginning they lay in bed in the shared room they'd found on Craigslist. Elise had decorated it with Gorsky and Rothko prints she found at a flea market. She swirled his chest hair. Their bodies nude. So do you want to quit your job? she asked. Do you want to move to Europe?

I don't think I could ever move there, but I could travel. For months, Elise; there's so much to see. And she agreed with a long kiss, which led them to the rest.

The parents needed a visit before leaving, so the young couple took a trip: first to Sioux Falls, then to Omaha. Paul was unsure how Mom and Dad would take the news, but they would have to admit they would've never approved of this trip in his early twenties, the age when most people went adventuring. He thought, too, with Elise in the passenger seat of her aging Altima, that maybe his parents would have a hard time denigrating his choices now that he had a woman validating everything he did.

JEFFREY ELLINGER

Having her implied, maybe even
demonstrated, that all the decisions that
had seemed wrong at the time—Alaska,
Nebraska, Austin, L.A., Minneapolis,
Seattle—were right. Strange then, Paul
thought as he drove: I am settling, and I
shouldn't be doing this. Though maybe,
he thought, that's what a man does if he
wants to be happy. He doesn't chase
after ones who say You're just not
country enough and Why are we still
going through this nonsense? Those
who comment on the mercurial spark.
People like that would always
disappoint. The one who slept soundly
in the front seat, hand on top of his,
would never intentionally harm anyone.
She had moved to Portland after
college, looking for new experiences the
Midwest could never offer. In Europe,
Paul thought, he could gain a broad
perspective and figure out what he could
do to finally make her and himself
happy. Once they got home he could
release Elise into the calmness of her
hometown, like a hooked fish put back
in a stream. For a moment on the drive
Paul forgot his yearnings. Elise slept. In
all the years before, driving by himself,
Paul had not been able to do what they
had done on the drive. He had not been
able to say, Look, there, at that, or sing
along with someone to the radio, or
receive a rub on his head when he got

tired. This is how driving should've always been, how he'd always wanted it to be. But only, Paul thought, if it were with someone I really wanted.

Elise woke and rubbed his leg and smiled. Her eyes closing again, her hand became still. Soon enough, they were in South Dakota.

Had it ever happened before? A man Paul's age bringing someone home for the first time? The first time for Paul was when he accompanied Elise through the garage door that led to the kitchen of his boyhood home. Mom had just taken out a batch of caramel popcorn, and both Paul and Elise would agree later that Mom seemed overcome with happiness as she gave Elise a tender hug, filling the room with the sense of home.

Come in, sit down, Mom said, her eyes wet. The house was so clean that it looked built for their arrival. The windows pulled open, a light breeze spilled in. The young couple munched on rolls and drank raspberry lemonade. The drive was okay then? Mom asked.

For sure, Paul said. Goes a bit faster with a buddy. And he gave Elise a friendly pat on her back.

I'm sure, Mom said. I'm sure it does.
From now on, she must have thought,
she would not have to worry about what
went on in her son's head. She would
not have to worry that he would
prematurely leave this world.

The rest of the Bethel family came over
that night, and everyone included Elise
as one of their own. That heartened
Paul, but in another way their affection
dismayed him, so he alternated between
showing Elise real affection and smiling
tight-lipped, reserving his real joy for
someone who must still, he thought, be
out there. They didn't stay long in Sioux
Falls, just long enough for Paul to show
Elise where he went to high school, at
Lincoln, and the Loop—where he drove
around with his friends in the late
nineties—and the Sioux Empire Mall,
the biggest one-story enclosed mall in
America, Paul said jokingly, but he
couldn't help but feel a flicker of pride
that Sioux Falls had something that
could stand up against anywhere else.
Elise held his hand as they browsed the
chain stores and her grip enveloped
him. On their last night Elise was
upstairs with Paul's mom, putting the
final touches on supper, while Paul
packed in his childhood bedroom.

So what's the plan then? Dad asked
from the doorway. You guys getting two
rooms? That's going to be awfully
expensive.

I doubt it, Dad, we'll probably sleep in
the same room. We couldn't afford to
get two rooms all the time, I don't think.

In the same room, Dad said, showing
not anger but disappointment. That's not
the best choice there, Paul.

Why is that? Paul asked, in a weak
show of defiance.

Take my word for it, Bud. I don't think
you want to go down that road.

Dad. I'll . . . But then Paul stopped,
knowing he could not tell his father that
Elise would bring along enough birth
control pills to last through the trip.
Everything was better left unsaid, like
it'd been for the last thirty or so years.
The women called down. Time for
dinner. Both men were thankful as they
left the basement for a home-cooked
meal. All together, no one would talk
about anything disagreeable.

JEFFREY ELLINGER

Paul and Elise left Sioux Falls the next day as a solidified pair, Paul thinking about how it'd now be harder to let her go. He didn't say as much as he drove south on I-29, and she didn't pry. That was not Elise's way. Mostly on the serene trip to her beginnings she paged through one of the guidebooks. She excitedly bookmarked places she planned for them to go.

Isn't life grand? Elise said, closing the book and placing it on her lap. Sunlight flickered through the clouds. It came through the car's windows at all kinds of dazzling angles. Paul only nodded.

Elise's parents lived in a nice suburb of Omaha, not that far from Warren Buffett, and the first thought Paul had when he met them was how much Elise looked like a younger version of her mom, and how much that worried him. The unfair thought made Paul feel guilty as he got to know Judith, who was friendly and warm. In the two days he spent in her home neither she nor Elise's dad asked what Paul would be doing with his life, nor did they seem alarmed at his lack of prospects. In fact, it was just the opposite. They were pleased to have Paul and gave him as many helpings of food and bottles of beer—since they drank—as he wanted. They even enjoyed the stories Paul told about his travels. How cute it was, they said, how Elise and Paul met. Judith and Gary went so far as to jokingly tell Paul that they wouldn't mind if he decided to stay in Omaha when he got back. If you need somewhere new, Judith said.

That night in Elise's childhood bed—her parents allowed such premarital behavior——Elise's head rested on Paul's chest as he imagined this room being the room he would come back to for holiday events and family reunions. He thought about how he would have to get used to the way Elise had arranged her childhood bedroom, the way it smelled, the old pictures from dance recitals and soccer practices and summer camps. He kissed Elise on the top of her head. Goodnight, he said. He disliked the smell of her hair, with residuals from the stubbornly ingrained organic shampoo she'd gotten back in Portland. Turning over, he lay awake for a long time.

Judith gave them a ride to the airport the day they left. Her vision blurred in the morning, so on the way they nearly got in an accident. Elise had her mom pull over and they switched for safety. At the

airport, Judith promised not to drive
again until things cleared up.

Oh, don't worry, Judith said, as her
daughter parked in the structure. I'll be
fine. My eyes just need to wake up a bit.

The three of them walked through the
short-term lot, and as they moved closer
to embarking on the biggest trip of their
adult lives, Paul and Elise looked
outmatched. The furthest either had
been out of the country was, for Paul,
Winnipeg, and for Elise, Guatemala, and
both had been mission trips.

They ate a small lunch at one of the
restaurants outside security. You two
are going to look like a couple of
hitchhikers in those backpacks, Judith
said. I don't understand how you're
going to have enough clothes for the
whole trip.

We're backpacking, Mom, Elise said.
We'll wash our clothes.

Paul smirked in solidarity. He had
wanted his trip to Europe to be all lavish
hotels and foreign guides feting him with
hearty feasts in the countryside. He had
wanted breakfast in bed and heavy
suitcases that bellhops brought up to his

room, but it would never be like that, and if he wanted to go he would have to cede to Elise's plans. So Paul had left her to hash out the pragmatics, which consisted of backpacks and going by train, bringing the barest of essentials. Yep, just the essentials, Paul said, and gave a little eye roll. Judith laughed, though Paul knew Elise was right. Sarcasm was his way of making it seem as if there were better decisions to be made.

Don't give me that, mister, Elise said. You know why we're doing it the way we're doing it. He knows, Mom. Don't encourage him.

Oh, all right, Judith said. As long as you two know what you're doing, we support you. Also, we wanted to give you two something. For the trip. Judith reached in her bag and took out several crisp cashier's checks. We want you to take this, she said, and insisted by opening Elise's backpack and stuffing them inside. Don't try to sneak them back to me, Elise. If you want, think of it as an early Christmas present.

Elise took a quick look, seeing the numbers printed on the check. Mom, it's so much. The women reached across

JEFFREY ELLINGER

the table and hugged. The money made
Paul feel like a failure, but he was so
moved by the gesture that he reached
out and hugged Judith too.

Don't spend it all in one place, Judith
said. And you have to send lots of
postcards and take lots of pictures.
Okay? That's the deal.

We will, Mom, Elise said, full of love. Of
course, we will.

Their parting was upon them. They had
their last goodbyes. Paul, forgetting
himself, hugged Judith once more, and
after he walked through the security he
looked back and saw not someone
else's mom, but his own, waving. And it
wasn't at all like they said it was, he
thought as he waved back. It was
actually, he would later think, kind of
wonderful.

After returning from their month-long
tour of Europe, things began to
deteriorate, though if either Paul or Elise
had ever been honest with themselves,
they could easily have traced the
erosion back to when they first met.
They'd forgotten how it had taken a year
of seeing each other nearly every week
for a romance to begin. A delay caused

not by shyness, but by a joint aloofness.
Inertia pushed them into a love where
every love for every person in the entire
world is played out, and this time it
happened to be theirs. Both Paul and
Elise would always be lonely people.
Together, their loneliness intensified.
Instead of appreciating Elise's studied
tips for traveling and her helpful
suggestions for what they should do
each day, her patient understanding for
his constant befuddlement overseas,
Paul could only resent that he had to be
backpacking for his big trip to Europe.
He didn't know her, the one who was
supposed to be there with him, but he
feared she lived in Nebraska or Texas
or California. Knowing she was
somewhere far away, Paul gave in over
the Atlantic Ocean. As a young Christian
Paul Bethel had envisioned his proposal
as a holy ceremony itself, overflowing
with flowers and devotional scriptures
and everything down on one knee.
Instead, Paul haphazardly went through
with it after they serendipitously had
their seats upgraded from economy to
first class for a marginal price. Reclined
next to Elise, her head on his shoulder,
Paul breathed in her smell. For nearly a
month Elise had not used her natural
shampoo or toothpaste, so he breathed
her in fully. Her hair had become wild
from not washing it, and she was fit and

had been good, never giving him a hard time for being lost or making him feel like less than a man for not having enough money to take them to the best restaurants after her parents' money ran out. From the window seat Paul woke Elise with a gentle push of his shoulder.

Honey, look. Paul pointed in the direction in which he thought Europe to be. Can you believe we were there?

Blankets over them, she snuggled closer, putting her hands under his shirt and on his warm belly. They stayed like that, and those moments high above the water were probably the most perfect ones Paul and Elise would ever have. So, he decided, now's the time, and it must have seemed to come to her through a haze. Elise, he said, I think we should get married.

Most everyone in the cabin slept. Only a couple of stray overhead lights, like lamps in a cave. Elise tended to be docile, but she dug her nails so hard into Paul's stomach she drew blood as she whispered yes in his ear. Paul kissed her. She channeled her hand under his waistband and pulled on his prick until he was spent. They both fell asleep. Later, Paul woke to an uncomfortable crustiness and thought about what his life would be like if Elise never woke again. The morbid thought made Paul almost ill, so he tried to come up with real options, actual plans, but the only thing that kept creeping up was his old strategy, and moving no longer seemed like an escape.

Not long after they returned Paul and Elise organized a wedding near her hometown of Omaha. And though the ceremony came close to what Paul once imagined—his bride wearing a white dress at an old church in the country, all his family attending and even some of his old married college friends, all with two or three small children—the reception was marked by awkwardness. Everyone from Elise's side of the family got drunk and so did Elise, to the point where Paul could hardly make eye contact with his own parents and aunts and uncles and cousins and grandparents, secluded in a corner of the outdoor tent, nervously sipping on pop and eating catered food. Seeing their discomfort caused more pain in Paul than he ever could have expected, and it was at his wedding that he realized how selfish he had been, moving around for so many years. That passed when Elise took his hand to dance. Paul saw his bride, all done up in

makeup, hair curled and styled, and felt
deeply sorry for himself, and for her,
knowing she looked as good as she
ever thought she could.

After the wedding they lived in Omaha
proper. Elise's family owned a
renovated three-bedroom in Benson that
awaited renters at a more than fair price.
So the young Bethel family moved away
from Portland, and in that home of theirs
in Nebraska they had two cats. One was
named Bing and the other Crosby, but
after Crosby ran away one morning—
Paul and Elise each blaming the other—
they had only Bing. As for the rest of the
memories from that time, their fondest
would be their first Christmas together.
Paul bought Elise a new bicycle, one he
wrapped with a red bow, like in holiday
television commercials for luxury cars,
while Elise made Paul a short film with
footage shot in Europe. They watched
on Christmas night, their stomachs full
with ham and wine, a peaceful snow
outside, the tree lit in the living room, hot
chocolate with liquor warming their
bellies, Bing at their feet, a blanket over
them, the fire, all of it so cozy, and Paul
was amazed at how many places they'd
gone and how well Elise had recorded
them all. She even narrated the video,
highlighting their mishaps and triumphs
against a soundtrack of songs they both

loved. It was more than enough to make Paul want to cry. He did not, though Elise did, and after it ended they made love, for one of the last times.

They divorced less than a year later, and since most of their affection had long drained they did not have a messy separation. Elise stayed in that house, and for all Paul knows she lives there still. One might think it strange things ended so abruptly and completely for them, but their love never grew, not like Paul once hoped it might, and seeing her again would only cause remorse, he knew, one redolent of all the wrong choices he made, of letting hope and desire steer his thinking instead of logic and reality. Elise had no reason to see Paul, either, so they never did. At the point of their divorce Paul had turned thirty-three, the same age as Christ when he died on the cross, a fact not lost on Paul, who did not take the advice of his parents to come home and see if a more conventional life could provide some much-needed direction. Paul instead chose to keep moving, as he'd always done. At some point in that listless future, while living alone in the Wisconsin suburbs after another left him, he wrote a long jeremiad on the state of his decrepit, long-abandoned faith.

JEFFREY ELLINGER

BALDING

**He has made my skin and my flesh
grow old and has broken my bones. -
Lamentations 3:4**

II

Is there any mercy left? No one can
afford clothes from a subscription box.
The gods must hate us if they devised a
system where everything we want is just
outside of our reach, and not today or
tomorrow but forever. This is how it all
works: good genes are passed down
and bad ones are passed down and if
you are lucky you are encoded with the
good ones and if you are unlucky you
are an anthropomorphized miasma with
a surfeit of ordure and every day wake
up thinking about how to stop waking up
with the same thoughts, like why is the
sky always gray, and who can afford a
nice outfit from a subscription box, and
even though you go to CrossFit you are
the exact same size. Our Lord is not like
the gentle and peaceful gods originating
from the four corners of wind and light
and rain and sun, like Black Elk says.
Our Lord does not acknowledge we are
here. Mark who once preached in

JEFFREY ELLINGER

Ballard tells us that our Lord hates us.
Right now, without a doubt, hate. Yes
our Lord would come down and end us
if He thought that would make us suffer
but our Lord knows the most suffering is
through living, so He allows us to
continue. How gray the sky. How tired
our eyes. There are so many books we
have not read, like that novel about an
aging music professor having sex with a
young Cuban student who is a
masturbatory surrogate for the author to
fill out his unfulfilled fantasies of making
love to a voluptuous Cuban woman he
taught fiction writing to in real life but
who would not go to bed with him. Okay,
yes, you have read that book but there
are so many others you have not and
you are not even sure if Robert the
auteur was that good or if Pauline the
critic just wanted to be different. Is
Transformers any better? Why not allow
glints of light to be art? Yes all things
are true and yes our Lord loves breasts
like a college bro. No torso or head or
lower half and every so often He tells
the breasts to get Him a sandwich from
heaven's kitchen and the breasts come
back with lunch resting on their buoyant
teardrops. Those big round areolas and
the pink nipples jutting out like thimbles.
Our Lord with His breasts for a wife has
told me to warn the world of its coming
doom as I sit in my living room

surrounded by Gnostic literature. I can see well from my chair as I play my soccer video game and grit my teeth in frustration that our Lord invented this game so I could fail until I submit to His will and know I am a speck of dust on an ant's back and He is as strong as infinite Hafþór Júlíus Björnssons. A conduit, a cipher, a vacuous pipe ready to be breathed into and blared through like an alphorn, with the sounds of my prophecy covering the land like a deep resonant flatulence. Also know that no one believes in what you're doing. How could they? You cannot focus, thinking about an acorn you kicked onto a lawn that you are now worried will be mowed over in winter and blind an innocent child. How lost our Lord has perfectly made you, to really identify with a film about intersectional feminism as a thirty-five-year-old heterosexual white male self-published author of autobiographical fiction. Hilarious. You think your struggle is the same as the struggle of the great artists? Everything is cold and gray but the earth is hot and you think putting yourself in a human-sized ice cube will help? Maybe that will allay the coming disaster for an eon or two, but what about when everyone dies from nuclear war and no one is around to refill the capsules with nitrogen? What about when the earth gets so hot even dry ice melts? What a frail creature, thinking you can listen to Televisionmind describe anything that's slightly creepy as Lynchian and love the writing of Paul with the bandana and not be as insufferable as someone who listens to Televisionmind and describes anything that's slightly creepy as Lynchian and loves the writing of Paul with the bandana. The hubris is all the more outstanding coming from someone who uses a word like "hubris." You think you are more special than you are. How else could you keep on living? Either you think you are going to be someone who helps figure out how to send the human race to other planets or you believe the Creator of everything chose you out of everyone in the history of everything to be with Him after you die to live forever in happiness while others are left behind to suffer. You have to choose one or the other to fight the nagging pulse that says you have evolved too far and know too much and in that too much is an absence. Complain about that, not about how you are losing your hair or about how your member is not as big as a black man's you saw in a video on your laptop or about how you could have written screenplays if you had been born with two screenwriters for parents or about how you too could have been called a voice for our time if

someone had given you a show on
premium cable after connecting with
studio heads who were friends with your
wealthy Manhattan sculptor parents.
Rage against that which is at least
somewhat productive to rage against:
the nothingness, and that you got that
nothingness idea from a fantasy movie
from your childhood with a horse that
may have died in the process of filming
such a sad, disillusioning film. You are
going to pass into darkness one day too
and all you have done will be forgotten.
Worry about that, and about how there
are dishes in the sink and clothes to be
put away and apartments to search for
and better jobs to want. Do not spend
time wondering why this person follows
that person online. Meditate on how we
are all microfibers in the shirt of life and
know that your metaphors are terrible.
That's why you will never become what
you want to become. When you go to
job interviews, you think, I'll just come
up with answers on the fly, believing
yourself smart enough to know what the
manager across from you will want to
hear, but when you get in there the only
words you know are "certainly" and
"obviously" and "strictly speaking," as if
all language has been boiled down to
those words and outside there is war
and disease and the distance of one
star from the other and there you are,

getting weepy about space. These are
your sins. Our Lord has not forgotten
them when He sees you at home
rubbing your member with lotion,
making that suction sound like macaroni
and cheese. Our Lord will punish you for
making that suction sound with your
body and thinking about other flesh He
created. Remember, when you were
married, you sinned by having thoughts
of other women. Now run your errands
and work at your bad job in data entry
after so many years of physical labor
and know that every single thing you do
is another layer to add on top of the
doberge cake that is your failed life.
There are people taking part in
movements for desperate peoples in
dangerous parts of the world and you
are in an apartment along a lake on land
stolen from Natives eating pizza and
worrying about your lack of social media
followers and whether or not you should
post a picture you took of dandelions in
the park. You should not, and yes the
people at your CrossFit class are talking
about you behind your back, about how
you can't do a pull-up. They think you
are too old to be working out at a gym
they call a box where all the college girls
wear shorts that stop right below their
big firm asses. Pathetic, how you signed
up for a clothing subscription box too,
and how many times in a day will you go

to the bathroom? Know our Lord put a bacterium in you that disrupts your flora so you are bound to the toilet. Spend every day, as our Lord has willed, wishing you are lither than you are, and each time you have an expulsion be deceived into thinking you are doing something with your time when really you are only releasing waste from your innards. The fat around your belly will remain until you expire and no one will come to visit your bones at Père Lachaise. No flowers will be laid at your grave. Even your waste, which could have been used as fertilizer, will be filtered and processed and eradicated. There are important events in the world while you have your hands down your pants waiting for someone to give you permission. Our Lord has given permission to those who call upon His Name and ask for His Power and Glory. Call upon Him and receive His Righteous Strength, or go and try on the clothing from your subscription box. This time, I'm sure, one of the garments will fit. You must have shrunk magically in the last five minutes. Our Lord could take away all your sorrow if He wanted to, but He wants to keep His special knowledge that He gave to angels who spoke to a man in a Utah desert with golden plates. If you could believe, you would be resplendent in your shining robes. Fifty more years until the Rapture now. "Dispensationalism" is a word that means everything. Someone conceived of the end and now it determines the future. And yes the punishment for your desires is that you must stay inside on a couch and create the fictive dream about failing. Bang your head against a wall until you no longer have a head but a neck gushing blood and still your brain will not shut off. The only way to shut it down is to go jump off a high structure, which is a sin that will send you to hell, where you will be separated from our Lord. You will have a forever of that, and that is the worst thing there can be, says anyone who takes the parts of the holy book they want to believe and thinks hell is not flame and fire and sulfur but internal introspection, like eternity in a coffee shop with a MacBook and a Bible but no yellow highlighter. Blasphemy, I say, as a prophet atop a steeple built by Germans in Wisconsin where I live after stops in many other cities, hell is fire and melting flesh and the smell that comes with trillions of bodies burning for eternity. A huge pile of misery for not choosing, when told as toddlers, the story of a man from thousands of years ago who killed trees and told His disciples to hate their mothers and fathers and who antagonized the ruling government until they killed Him but

later came back to life and who is also
the one who came up with the idea for
blobfish and hurricanes and quasars.
That's our Lord, but there are other
lords, like the lord who tells His followers
to kill unbelievers so they can have sex
with virgins for eternity and the lord who
calls the people He loves the chosen
people. They cannot allow anyone else
in their group unless one enrolls in
classes, and that takes years, and even
then all the other chosen ones know that
new person is not a real chosen one by
the way he looks and his last name. An
example, you ask. Okay, think about
this. How many girls have you met who
even though only their father is chosen
still claim they are part of the special
chosen club? Many, because they want
the artistic and/or intellectual reputation
and to one day inherit a great sum of
money. All these worldviews are true
and right and should be taken seriously
and you should pray five times a day
and sit shiva. All these exclusive clubs,
we must hold on to them, our Lord
commands, so as to retain our sense of
tradition and war, so as to set
boundaries and create industry.
Economies are based on families
receiving a stipend for having a father or
son in a club's killing group, and since
that is the only job in some poor areas
of the world, the families are glad to

have a brother or uncle who beheads journalists or controls bombs that fall out of planes onto cities. Stop now. A pit grows in your stomach. Sense the silence emanating from the apartment. Our Lord wants you to be lonely after years of conceited moving during which you followed your own selfish whims. The arrogance, thinking yourself a sensitive writer who should be recognized. You think a word like "solipsism" describes your autobiographical fiction but you don't know how to pronounce "solipsism." Throw yourself on a pit of flames and perhaps our Lord will save you from the fire eating away at your flesh throughout time. But I doubt He will. You would count the burning as another one of your troubles and write about it as the paper burns. Right now you could be contributing to the world but you continue with your vain project instead. You think, If I keep going, good things will happen. Our Lord did not destine you for good things. He destined you to strive for years and die without ever reaching your dreams. Past the age where you should have made it, you have not moved to New York and written a script in less than a month at a movie star's cabin. If a movie star saw you today, he or she would think, I'm glad that drone exists. He makes it

possible for me to be a star. With all the
drone money pooled together, my
movies are a hit, and the drones are
entertained for a couple hours before
they go back to their drone lives where
they have to carry their laundry to a
separate building then carry that
laundry, wrinkled and unfolded because
they don't have the time, back to their
apartments. The drones go to a day job
and at night work on their sad projects.
I'm glad drone people exist, the star
says. The best part of your drone night
is the free cookie at Subway. Now a
hex, a pox, a disease on you for your
impatience with the tattooed worker who
stuck his tongue out in concentrated
silence as he made you a sandwich.
Shame on you. The worker makes less,
and his road is more steep, and you
could not muster the patience to give a
hello when he did not serve you in the
amount of time you thought
appropriate? Your cookie is now worms
and sand and no longer macadamia nut,
the kind you ate as a boy with the ones
who loved you and wanted the best for
you. Tremble with fear when you go to
bed and know there are millions who
believe you are going to burn eternally
for not believing in our Lord and His
prophet, just as there are millions of
others who believe those people—and a
billion more who worship animals—will

JEFFREY ELLINGER

burn eternally for not believing in
another prophet. Our Lord has willed
this. He is good because He says He is
good. The screams of burning are only
there to distract you from your projects
at night, which are very important, I
preach sarcastically. The worst part is
you thinking someday something will
break. Yes, there are those who have
made it, but have you ever stopped to
wonder how they did? Our Lord
destined them, and still you go home
and hammer away in the garage or turn
on your camera to film yourself putting
on makeup, or you program an app that
will never get the proper venture
capitalist to catapult you into tech-bro
heaven. Stop the useless striving. Even
for the chosen ones born with success
bred into their marrow, their ascendance
to the top of their field—which they think
they chose but was laid out for them at
the moment their mother's egg received
their father's whipping flagellum—does
not matter. All accolades and monies
turn to dust. Only heaven and hell
remain. Repent, insignificant child with
no chance, or let this all drift to the back
of your mind and eat your sand. Soon
your flesh will be off your body. Sit on
the couch expressionless and unable to
compose anything interesting. The snot
will run down your philtrum as you think
of how to pronounce "elegiac." Your

tongue is useless and you are helpless
and an underwhelming lover. Our Lord
has willed this. Do not try to wriggle out.
You do not live in a fantasy movie where
the villain ties the rope loosely and you
can cut the binds with a paper clip
hidden in your pocket. This is the world
and you are in it and there is no
escaping. You are not Paul who
righteously bedded Bathsheba. Our
Lord chose that Paul to be with the thick
yoga teachers with underarm hair of his
day. Also, it is our Lord's plan that you
never hold a baby panda. He made it so
you cannot complete the requisite
science courses to become a zoologist,
and He did not give you the bravery
required to venture into the wilds of the
Qinling Mountains to see them for
yourself. Our Lord did not want you to
have a forest of bamboo in your
backyard, so you cannot entice the
bears to forage for the hundreds of
pounds they need to gain a fraction of
nutrition. That was all part of our Lord's
plan, His divine board game we are all
pieces within, and if lucky we get to be
the thimble and not the wheelbarrow,
tipping over and uselessly small. Now
listen to praise and worship music. Lift
your hands in the air. If you are able to
lift your hands the highest and keep
them up the longest, know you are
secure in our Lord. If you cannot, how

are we to know where you stand? Listen
to the drums behind the plastic cage,
beating in rhythm with the pulse of our
Lord. Yes, you now want the leftover
pizza in the refrigerator, but if you were
built with a body that liked eating healthy
and working out, you would not. I know
this because I know the before and the
after. I have been to the beginning and
the end. I am close with the Alpha and
the Omega. Remember, nothing has
anything to do with how hard you work
but with how your mother's egg met
your father's sperm. All toiling is vain.
Enroll in an online fiction workshop. You
are not leading the online fiction
workshop. Our Lord determined at your
birth that you'll one day have self-
published autobiographical fiction no
one will read and when you go to the
fridge on another forgotten day all you
will want is pizza even though you just
ate an apple and could stand to lose
fifteen pounds but all you can think
about is pizza. Not because you are
weak—though you are—but because
this was all written by our Lord in your
story billions of years ago. Going
shopping for clothes on the weekend will
not help your cause. No matter how
many tough shirts from Seattle or denim
jeans from North Carolina or boots from
London or watches from Detroit or
cameras or leather journals you buy—all

laid out in a neat grid and displayed on
social media—your body will be the
same and the dark circles under eyes
will remain and the fat on your belly too.
All your failures will be in your past,
dangling above your head like a mobile
over a baby's crib, spinning and gaining
appendages as time marches on. Make
plans and sell possessions and create
lists and do push-ups and read books
and learn languages. You will be the
same pile of flesh, staring at your
phone, waiting for an update. You are
not in tune with nature enough to be
with an earthen fairy with armpit hair
who lounges around all day and posts
masturbation videos and goes to self-
discovery workshops. You will have
someone who has to work too much to
make up for your deficiencies. Worry
about your phone now. Where is it? Is it
okay? Does it have enough battery? Our
Lord has decreed your hellish fate. How
harsh, the sinner proclaims! No, says
our Lord, who knows every tweet from
people you don't like is annoying and
that nearly every creative work made
available to the public is a sham and
that you are only capable of worrying
about your phone. Our Lord wants you
to stare at your phone now and become
a pillar of salt. How cliched you are, in a
coffee shop next to others who lean
across their table to kiss. If you had

been chosen to work at a good job by
our Lord you would own your own home
with your Spanish handball-champion
wife and live there with a busty college-
aged au pair and on weekends have
passionate threesomes at an upscale
hotel. If you could think of stories with
detectives in countries with characters
who know the customs and languages
and local brands of furniture, you'd have
that life, but you are in a coffee shop,
and you are not even writing. You are
sipping cappuccino, but you don't know
what a cappuccino is. You only ordered
a cappuccino to sound like someone
who knew what to order and now you
are worrying that the music in your
headphones is too loud and whether
you tipped enough at the restaurant last
night, if it should have been five dollars
or six. Six would have been too
generous, but giving that extra dollar
would have let you live with a carefree
mind. Our Lord made you this way, to
be bogged down with misfiring neurons,
tied like a bad shoelace tangled in
earbud cords. That's how He wants you
to be, and so you shall be. And yes you
realize what a booty can do, it can
incapacitate you, but what else do you
know? Learn from our Lord that a man
lives inside a whale's stomach for some
time but the man never dies. The
enzymes in a big fish's stomach never

erode skin, when you believe. Also learn
that if someone who believes takes his
only son up a mountain with the purpose
of killing him with a knife, right before
the murder our Lord will intervene and
say, Okay, that's enough, you took your
son up that mountain and were about to
take a sharp rock to his stomach, but
you stopped in time and that proves you
believe in me. Another good thing to
know is that our Lord tells a man
through brain waves that the entire earth
will flood, which prompts the man on
earth to construct a gigantic boat to hold
all the world's animals. The animals get
hypnotized and walk thousands of miles
to board a vessel and are saved from
the waters that drown everyone else,
including small children, whom our Lord
hates. That one man who heard the
whispers is saved, along with his family,
and they have incest with one another
until they repopulate the earth. There
are so many more lessons, important
ones to show you how you are chosen,
like happy Paul, or not chosen, like poor
Judas or Cain. Paul was chosen and
Lot's wife was not. Peter was and
Jezebel was not. Abraham was and
Herod was not. Do you get it now? If
you want to know if you are chosen, ask
yourself three questions. Do you speak
to our Lord in public? Do you pray
constantly? Have you been to the

ancient city of Thessalonica? All
heathens care about is seeing the
sunset in Santorini but Santorini is not in
any of the holy scriptures. All the while
you are in a coffee shop and there is
nothing else you could be doing right
now other than worrying about your
phone's battery life. Do that now. Burn
later. The penalty of your moving and
divorcing and not settling on a career is
baldness, and your baldness is why you
work in a cubicle where your lisp is
mocked by your boss who switches from
joking to professional when it suits her.
She describes how much sex she wants
with men who are not her wimpy
husband then snaps into a veteran
office-worker when she needs to. Your
baldness and average lovemaking give
you the lack of confidence needed to
settle for a job where the assistant to
your boss speaks to you like a piece of
dirt. Your lack of a graduate degree has
put you in a place where you get a sick
feeling in your stomach thinking of the
next time you have to go to work. Do not
fear, this is our Lord doing great work in
you. He wants to see your resolve, now
that you are older. He wants to see how
long you can go before you end
yourself. You would have done so much
good for the world if you had lived in
New York in your twenties while
churning out scripts for movies shot in

black and white or done stand-up for
years in Los Angeles, honing your
craft—instead of driving around
delivering goods—and now you could
be in one of those streaming dramas
where all the lines are on point, written
by one of your heroes, who masturbated
in front of aspiring comediennes and
made those surrealist movies that are
now so revered and hard to find that just
one copy can cost thousands of dollars.
Thousands upon thousands, those are
the numbers of years our Lord does not
understand. Of all the things our Lord
can do—make something out of nothing,
send one man to eternal burning and
another to eternal bliss, send His own
Son who is Himself to die in the material
world—He cannot understand time. One
day is like a thousand to our Lord, and
that is not close. Usher is only two years
older than you, but to our Lord Usher
could be two thousand years older, yet
you are thinking about how much Usher
has done and how little you have done.
But our Lord wants Usher to have dance
moves and that line that goes from his
hip bone down to his pelvis. That is how
our Lord made Usher, to be able to do
that pivot dance where it looks like he is
moving but really he is swimming his leg
in place. Do not become low. Our Lord
has no idea how much older Usher is
than you. To Him, Usher could be a

million years dead in a sarcophagus in Egypt and you could be one of the slaves who made his pyramid. Through all millennia you are a shred of a piece of straw, meant to pull your follicles out while breaking your back so as to make a great place of rest for men our Lord handpicked. He placed you in that cubicle. Shovel the dung. Later it is night after the cubicle job and you are up, trying to make something of your life at home. Take a break every other sentence and browse for clothes you cannot afford. Check scores of baseball games you are not involved in. Look at your phone again. You have not heard a ding of reinforcement because our Lord wants you to have no dings. Now our Lord wants you to look up the best ratio of home runs to runs batted in and after that get waylaid by a video of a ballpark reporter who wears red lipstick and a gray blazer and holds a phallic microphone that gets knocked out of her hand by a baseball. She is thick and attractive and blonde and seems at first surprised and then perturbed that someone would have the audacity to allow her to be embarrassed. She and others have lived privileged lives, and it is good you have not. You are white and straight and male and no one will believe you are not doing exactly what you want to do all the time. Feel how hot

your living quarters are now. You do not
have air flowing through your apartment.
Cool air is being used elsewhere for
higher purposes. Our Lord wants the air
to be that way. There was a battle for
that air and also for your soul that has
been won or lost. If you wanted to burn
eternally, you have won. Otherwise, you
have lost. But maybe everything will turn
out well and burning will be good, like
being wrapped in a wool blanket on a
winter day instead of your skin peeling
off from the singeing of an iron until it
reaches your bones and starts all over
again. Now go drink some whiskey and
eat some bacon and enjoy yourself in
the limited time left on this mortal plane.
A few years of yearning with the
subsequent guilt until our Lord is
merciful and has you ended so you can
enjoy an infinity of lava in your mouth.
His love endures. Sit and journal your
obscenities while eating ten dollars'
worth of tea that is mostly ice and a
sandwich of mostly lettuce in a coffee
shop beside men who wear all black
and jack it to pictures of old girlfriends
on Facebook in the bathroom while their
wives watch their children in the living
room. The logical subsequent yelping is
filtered through earbuds so the sounds
do not go through the bottom crack of
the door, and every so often there is a
turning of the handle, but the men are

smart and have learned they must lock the door if they want privacy. Sit by those men in the coffee shop and know in the beginning our Lord wanted to give you more. He sketched for you a great blueprint, but time has no meaning for our Lord, so as you began to experience life you began to muddle up the perfect plan our Lord had for you. He wanted to give you concubines waving palm fronds, suckling on your testicles as others engulfed your significant prick. Yeshua and Allah and Buddha all wanted that. They did not want you smashing your member to the forms of naked women with hairy armpits and pointed breasts on a computer but impregnating them and springing forth more creatures. Our Lord wanted so many more of you made in His image, and the way to do that would have been by bedding Asians and redheads and Jews and Persians and tanned models who pose almost nude on hiking trips in Utah for their curated social media. Those our Lord had planned for you, but you undid it all. Our Lord could not have undone anything. Our Lord is perfect. If our Lord wanted to He could imbue into you every single piece of knowledge, along with the required fuel units, to live a utopian blameless life of constant pleasure, but He does not want that. He wants you in that coffee shop beside the

businessmen talking ill about their
company receptionist, scheming to
divorce their wives, who stayed with
their men after weddings officiated in a
church where a cousin repeated that
epistle in Colossians, after which they
took separate candles and lit one in the
middle and the pastor said, Now the two
have become one and let no man put
asunder. These wives are not wishing
they could be with someone else,
because their men are important and
drive an Infiniti and are also on Tinder
secretly, having never used, as they call
it to friends, a dating website. Our Lord
wants you there beside those men. He
wants you to be on earth when all the
reefs are bleached and killed, when all
the tiger sharks have nowhere to go,
when all the pandas stop trying. Also
know you will never have a book of
esoteric poetry published by a chosen
man in a great Manhattan skyscraper
that features a poem titled "Esoteric"
that is a list of the groceries you bought
to make smoothies. That alt time is gone
and not coming back and you were
never a part of it. Our Lord did not want
you to be a part of the molesting
literature boys in Brooklyn, and not
because He has something grander
planned but because He has nothing
planned for you. Stop, insolent, a
servant does not question the master. A

servant enjoys his under-eye bags.
Accept what is in a chapter from a book
written by those who once anointed
themselves the chosen people in a time
when the invention of toilet paper would
have been shocking. Those chosen
people wrote the most sacred texts that
explain everything about the world
thousands of years later. Most of that
book the chosen ones wrote in a time
when people worried when the sun
disappeared every night. You must
believe in that book and use it to guide
every decision now. Use it to make the
people who don't follow the book guilty,
but more so it should make the people
who do try and follow all of the book
guilty when they don't. Guilt should be a
constant feeling, if you are in love with
our Lord. Also know there is no bardo,
where the sin falls off like scales as we
ascend. You can only be in the
presence of young men having sex with
teenage virgins after serving in the best
way by killing those who did not believe.
Yes, some of the noises the virgins
make are theatrical, our Lord thinks, like
can they really love it that much? But He
is glad His servants are enjoying
themselves. What lovely scriptures He
gave His people to read and understand
and follow. Before His books there was
Adam and Eve in the garden talking
directly with our Lord. They did not have

need of burdensome instructions to haul
into coffee shops with a highlighter.
They only needed apples and snakes
and greenery. Imagine that first member
and those first breasts, how supple and
heavy they must have been. Now stop,
as you have sinned and will burn. It's
true our Lord operates in unpredictable
ways, but He wants the best for you, if
you are one of His children, and we are
all His children, except for those who
are not and are to roast in hell forever.
Phil, a chosen one, made a career out
of writing pretend stories about his real
life bedding gorgeous women. Our Lord
willed that after dozens of self-obsessed
novels Phil would go to heaven—after
feasting upon young women with round
asses, putting his semen over their
warm bellies and young breasts, even
as an older married man, heaving and
sweating and exerting over them, and
they allowed this because they wanted
to know what it felt like to sleep with the
most powerful writer in the world, who
commanded million-dollar advances for
words no one read outside of those who
went to used bookstores on Saturday
afternoons and had a certain author who
started their search. So shall it be, says
our Lord. In your coffee shop now there
is a large man with a gray beard who is
tan like a lizard. He is only muscle and
emitting an aura of leather and talcum

powder around his balls. This man can recite full passages from the Book of Romans. Also, by the way, I did not tell you, I am Paul in heaven and decided to write a book for the modern times but this time without the subterfuge, just the facts. I did not choose for our Lord to strike me blind on that path to beat up His followers. Honestly, if He had not intervened, I would have spent the rest of my days happily taking a club to the faces of those who claimed there was someone who called himself our Lord. (Sorry, a quick diversion. I am cloaked as another man in a coffee shop and there is someone in here with curly hair and a stacked body with an ass that is so tight and round I am biting my knuckles. Luckily, our Lord neutered me so I cannot take further steps, but she keeps on getting up and if I could just be a dead fly on her chair so that when she came back from the bathroom she would sit on me, that would be even more wonderful than heaven. Please do not tell our Lord this.) As Paul, I want to tell you that another of your sins is being an amateur. How do you become not an amateur? Be born with skills and money for private schooling so you can call other people amateurs, like guys in their late thirties with beards on their necks and bags under their eyes who review candy on their YouTube channels and have other videos about their knife collections. Gather from the tinny production and bare apartment that the amateur man majored in philosophy but never made it past the second semester and his favorite books include the objectivist novel *Icarus Leaped* and a number of tomes, as he calls them, on how to survive in the wilderness. He lives in Colorado and has an ex-girlfriend who really, as he tells it, fucked him over, and he makes it seem like at any moment he could go live in the woods but he always gives up beforehand. The life you have where you sit and judge that man is not better. Our Lord does not love you more than He loves that totally bald man who has not had a job other than landscaper for the last five years and by the time he is forty-five will not be able to find work that pays him more than forty thousand a year. You are both animals in a pen, eating from a trough, pissing into bowls. Both of you are subject to your body's compunctions. You cannot say when you will go here or there just as the wind cannot say when it will blow. Listen now. Is it loud and hollowing or gentle and whirring? Do you feel a cool breeze, or is the air stifling and humid? Writing about the wind is like writing about high school. Bad artists do it when they can't come up with anything true. And you, as

an example of a bad artist, do not know
the definition of the word "genuflect."
You have used it incorrectly for years,
thinking it meant "reflect" because it
rhymed. How hilariously stupid you are.
Our Lord made you this way to show
you how much He loves you. How
wonderful too, considering what
"genuflect" means: to bend one knee in
deference to someone else. All this time
you believed to genuflect was to reflect.
How self-involved. Know this as well:
our Lord designed the human a certain
number of years ago but He cannot
remember how many. He sculpted the
minuscule bodies like one does with
clay, and once He connected them all to
the infinity server they blinked their eyes
and their operating systems whirred and
all life began. So unfathomable, to think
it happened any other way, to think
someone would write hundreds of pages
and call the pages sacrosanct because
they were chosen and a long time later
another person would come along and
write more pages of commentary on
those holy scriptures in a stream-of-
consciousness rant disguised as Paul.
Insanity, that would be. All trees will
evaporate when heaven and earth are
laid bare and in that time our Lord will
be laughing as He sets everyone on fire.
Jesus and Mohammed will be holding
hands. Knowing all that, get up and go

to work in a cubicle near fairgrounds in the Wisconsin suburbs and be nothing because that is what you are meant to be. I do not preach eugenics. I preach the word of our Lord. Please know you are crazy by the number of pages you have written that are not published. Put down your hopes and go look over old emails from former girlfriends, from back when you were lithe and had a head full of hair and your faith stood at its strongest. There is no sacrilege. All religions go straight to our Lord. The sacrifice of one man was for all, except for those who never heard of our Lord or who grew up in a culture where He was not the dominant figure, in which case there is only fire. I write all this from a soft bed in the room of college students I met at a coffee shop. There are four of them and their bodies are tan except for their bottoms and tits. I return to them while you must meditate and be saved. Our Lord loves those who think about Him all the time and never stop praying and kill themselves for His holy causes. As a postscript, remember how in your late teens and early twenties you scoured message boards for pictures of half-naked women because you were too afraid to be so bold as to search for naked women? You cannot think about that, as you are now thinking about how video games are made. How there are

JEFFREY ELLINGER

people in charge of transposing an
emotion onto a digital face using a
mouse and keyboard and drawing with a
pen on an electronic surface so as to
create a character that exemplifies said
emotion in a short scene, among
uncountable other scenes, in a narrative
filled with space beasts and alien races
and human-cyborg hybrids. All the while
you sit in your apartment thinking about
your sorrowful life as you are
simultaneously invested in a world
crafted over years by engineers and
artists and programmers who make
more in a day than you do in a year.
This is your lot, as determined by our
Lord. Your sin is that you now search for
naked women on your phone, looking to
find a yoga instructor who started her
own special practice on a farm outside
Madison where she shares her
wholesome breasts and unmanicured
auburn field. She debases herself to
show her dad he isn't in charge of her
anymore. Now you are thinking I am
being crass. But our Lord has told me I
must be strict to bring you back to the
fold, though He is already aware of who
is and is not going to come back to the
fold, and you never are. Still, He wants
me to try. That's how much He loves
you. Now you are wondering why it is
that black lives matter or why white lives
matter. Under the Lord, all lives matter,

except for the ones He has doomed to hell for eternity. Oh, but you say, those people who burn chose with their human will to turn away from the Lord and into sin, and you are right, they did, and now they will be on fire forever after they die. That is the right amount of punishment for not accepting the existence of an invisible judge of all actions ever. All lives matter. All knives scatter. All pies splatter. These are rhymes, but I did not think of them. Our Lord came up with them for me and picked up my fingers with His perfect hands. He used me as a puppeteer uses a marionette and plopped my fingers down on the keys in the right order using His heavenly grace and wisdom. A scooter honks in the distance. A grapevine in Italy ripens. A man outside will not stop coughing. These things are not related. I only mention them to be included in this holy book. Yes, there are many bad men with lots of hair in the world getting good things, but what does that have to do with you? Fates are for our Lord to mete out among His cherished creatures. Do you really think it possible for nothing to come from something? The invisible gas that emits from your body had to come from somewhere. Now a star dies a billion miles away and gives life to another earth, where our Lord has been forgotten and everyone lives in peace.

JEFFREY ELLINGER

Society has advanced and there is no
social media. Everyone eats pork
smoked on pimento bark and other
savory meats from a conch. Tribal
women dance rhythmically on the laps
of contented alien men. All is well.

JEFFREY ELLINGER

Those names not found written in the book of life were thrown into the lake of fire. - Revelation 20:15

III

Tribal women dance rhythmically on the laps of contented alien men. All is well. Paul Bethel had finished his jeremiad on religion. Unsure of the existence of a literary journal that would accept the unhinged screed, he found himself, rather than satisfied with finishing something, wanting. He looked beyond his glowing screen into the darkness of the apartment along the cold lake of a rusted city in Wisconsin. Is it better to write for your soul and have no public, he mused despondently, or to write for the public and have no soul? Cyril Connolly had thought the same thing a century before, but Richard Yates was the most obscure author Paul had ever heard of as he strained to hatch the beginning of his first published novel, the one he'd been trying to get down on paper for years but instead kept chronicling his repeating anxieties, the roundest backsides he'd known, the jobs he'd hated, all the wrong moves he'd made, the acceptable sums of money he'd never earned, the math he was bad at, the faith he'd left, and now, in these modern times, all the petty online dramas.

Or should it be a screenplay? Paul wondered. A blank page in front of him. The windows of his small apartment shook from the strong February winds. Darkness, except for his screen's glow. As a way of pumping himself up, Paul searched and found from the social media profile of a famous quasi-feminist Polish-American supermodel in Los Angeles that she was dating a bald man, and what greater carrot, he thought, to keep him striving than to know that a very famous quasi-feminist Polish-American supermodel in Los Angeles was dating a bald man? A bald man who, in the selfies Paul stalked, wore hats and overalls and had bright-green eyes. A self-proclaimed handsome man, this guy owned a record company and lived in Los Angeles. Those factors added to the equation, but the man could not subtract the baldness. Maybe, Paul thought, any bald or balding guy could make himself good enough for a world-class model by buying hats and wearing overalls in winter. Paul refocused. What should this be about?

After a peripatetic twenties and thirties, Paul had settled in the Middle West, and in the Middle West he would stay. Living up the river—as a real novelist once referred to anywhere outside of New York City—was fine by Paul, who believed he did not need to live in an important city to be important. He liked being different, and trying to make a living as a creative outside of New York was that. More accurately it was difficult, as Paul had built up his world to be, so that when he flamed out he could say, I just didn't give myself a true chance. That was the problem all along. In reality, bearded guys and privately educated women in Minneapolis and Seattle, even Fargo and Cleveland, wrote for a living. What really distracted Paul was his lady leaving him earlier that day, around three in the afternoon. A few hours before that, at lunch, she had eaten a sandwich, and for a solid minute Paul had stared at her, but she'd concentrated on her food and her phone as if in the room alone. Rattling of the windows now. Paul's lady did not mention coming back. They'd met at Tyler Novena's wedding in Chicago a year before, and Paul moved to be with her in Wisconsin around the time his balding accelerated. Now, on the day his lady left, Paul's coverage had dwindled to a few brave seedlings on top, holding on for dear life.

This has to be about more than balding, Paul said out loud to no one. Domestic trysts? He threw that out into the careless universe. Self-obsessed autobiographical novels would never sell, Paul thought next. A handsome bearded Norwegian had sated everyone's appetite for that six times over. Now consumers of online content wanted videos of beautiful multiracial actresses dancing to new songs by transgendered deejays who grew up quotidian in Akron or Sacramento but ended up in Brooklyn. They wanted rainbow-colored youths in Paris using gender-neutral pronouns. Paul could not write their story, yet he knew his novel would have to be about more than balding after his lady left him if he wanted to make money, and he would need money, as she had been the main breadwinner.

Divorce is everyday stuff, Paul said, once more to no one. No one wants to pay to watch everyday stuff.

JEFFREY ELLINGER

And Paul was right. No one would. They would pay to watch cartoons about pigeons living in New York City, whose trailer before Sundance features a psychedelic Satin Overland song, and that show is shopped around by high-powered agents, and a prodigal cable startup pays the highest price, and all the young ingenues stab each other in the backs for a chance to audition. Paul had lost focus while rattling off his reasons for not starting to write. How do the same unfunny actors keep getting cast in the same movies? he wondered. How do the bald ones get work?

Paul only knew this much: there can only be one bald man in an ensemble comedy about making it as a comedian in New York, just as there can only be one larger-than-average woman in the romantic movie set in Los Angeles with the big budget and shiny production values, just as there can only be one man on the couch in Wisconsin whose lady has left him after unsuccessful years of balding and failing and moving and driving around delivering goods and is now working in a cubicle near the fairgrounds and blaming all his balding on God.

But there are no novels about balding,
Paul repeated to keep going, or to at
least stay awake. On another afternoon
he sat at his warped desk from the
Martha Stewart Collection, a blank Word
document open on his computer, after
entering data in a cubicle in a building
near the fairgrounds and listening to his
coworkers rehash inchoate stories of
their kids, talk about their cramps, and
retell fatuous dreams of the night before.
Paul had self-published two short
autobiographical novels, and the next
one would take years, assuming he
could make it ready, and he had
promised himself to never self-publish
ever again, which meant he would have
to find an agent and a publisher, and
how long would that take, Paul
wondered. Years upon years he did not
have. Maybe, Paul thought without
hope, if he'd started submitting when he
first began to go bald after college,
things would be different now. But, as a
youth, the losing of his hair reduced his
thinking to a narrow slit, through which
only the most essential light could pass:
There's a hot girl in the student union,
God forgive me for looking at her,
please don't make me balder.

Outside Paul's ground-floor apartment,
the city tried. That, Paul's lady who'd left
once said, would be a good motto:

JEFFREY ELLINGER

We're Trying. A slogan for somewhere
that wants to be more than what it is, but
like Houston has its Austin and Atlanta
its Athens, Milwaukee had its Madison.
The problem, Paul reasoned, was that
the city had lost its soul, and now as it
moved into the next century tried to
construct one out of tapas restaurants
and tech startups and brewery tours and
brick buildings that used to be mattress
factories now converted into luxury
condominiums. That brand of
shoehorning made Milwaukee all the
sadder, in Paul's view. He wanted the
city planner and marketing team to go
back to building a beer town of sausage
and lederhosen. At least then they'd be
authentic, he thought, in their social
engineering. Paul, alone in the
apartment before his computer, balded
as he struggled to construct worlds for
two imaginary men, Mike and Tyler.
What would they be doing? Paul
wondered, but wrote nothing as he
looked at his phone. No likes or
favorites from any of his tepid followers,
so he procrastinated by thinking about
Milwaukee, and his balding, how it
looked worse as he watched a video of
himself reading from his latest self-
published novel, recording his
performance for consumption online
where the video would eventually
receive twelve views. After entering data

in the cubicle in West Allis and recording
the video in the apartment along the
lake, Paul sat at his desk from the
Martha Stewart Collection, assembled
by himself, and tried to think of the
definitions of the following words:
pernicious, forestall, insouciant. He
could not think of definitions for any of
them. And he had failed at pronouncing
"championing," stumbling while looking
into the camera. He started over several
times before acquiescing to never
getting it right. Birds sounded. Bars
covered the windows. Paul yanked,
tearing out a bundle of nose hairs. His
eyes watered. At work that day Paul had
dreamed of selling his car and moving
down to Mexico like authors did in the
fifties. Tramp his way and later there
would be a memoir about the
experience, with a majority of the
composing done on a sailboat while
working as a deckhand on the way to
Seitan Limania. Free to do as he
pleased, Paul looked to be on the verge
of weeping as he got up and went
around and smelled her remains in the
apartment: a pillowcase, the air in the
kitchen where she'd kept her toaster
and espresso machine, and in her
closet, going in and back out to regain
its plain fragrant scent, soapy and clean
.Mexico and Greece, both out of the
question; Paul needed to start his opus

on balding that featured two fictional men, one modeled after Mike. A year older than Paul, Mike lived in Minneapolis and owned a tech company. Once a proselytizing Christian, Mike had turned into a fierce atheist and now dated a nondenominational church-going Born Again after being hypnotized by her breasts during a drunken night of karaoke. Paul based the other character on Tyler. A year younger than Paul, Tyler began buzzing his hair in his mid-twenties and was now fully bald in his early thirties. A doctor now, tall and lean, Tyler looked not unlike a long penis. He'd cheated on his wife while he lived in Chicago and she lived in Charleston for her first year of medical school. They produced a child. As a bald married man with a baby, Tyler received sexts from college girls and graduate students and marketing interns, all of which Paul liked to imagine for himself, so that all that mattered was what you did and how much you made. The amount of hair on your head, Paul dreamed, mattered only to conceited girls who associated baldness with their grade-school gym teacher. Paul sat at the desk from the Martha Stewart Collection, its fake wood peeling, and tried to hemorrhage emotions onto his computer so as to illuminate the plight of the straight white balding man in America in the twenty-first century. The tip of his finger possessed a metallic scent from picking bloody snot from his nose. His lady had left and taken with her the lap dog Paul always said got in the way but now missed. Up in space, two bald men spun aimlessly, like bowling balls bumping into each other in an endless lane for eternity.

—

Paul thought about balding after another day entering data, sour after jokingly telling his favorite coworker and only friend at work to suck it in reference to the grade she gave him on his day's work of entering numbers. She'd given him a B-plus, while the two big mamas—longtime cubicle employees who did not like Paul—both gave sarcastic A-pluses. They laughed when he said suck it, and he apologized right away, but still Paul worried, after taking a turn in the city, that he'd caused the car behind him to disappear. For all Paul knew, that driver had been vanquished from the earth. At his cheap Martha Stewart Collection desk, Paul kept on being reminded of the car that may or may not have fallen into hell, and there was also the problem of someone whistling in the hallway. Paul wanted to yell shut up, but he did not. He sat there listening to the unfocused noises until they faded into another afflicted area of the world. Paul pulled up a picture of his lady, who was gone. There'd been a time when she would have thought enough of her man to pick out a thong and yoga pants, alter the lighting in the room, and snap a series of photos intended to capture a luscious version of herself, accentuating the generous curve from her smooth back to the outcropping of her healthy backside. Before she left she watched Paul eradicate them all, but he did have a secret backup. He could sense in the days leading up to her departure that she would erase every inch of herself. Now, in the intervaled silence—interstitially filled by the cawing of crows in the rock garden outside the barred windows and beyond that the humming of the traffic on Prospect—Paul could find no reason to try another take of him reading into a camera from his self-published autobiographical novel about online dating, or the other novel, about a CrossFit coach who makes love to all his students, or even start yet another, this time about balding.

Crown died today, Paul thought, fearing
that all the Important Creatives online
would spoil even the best artist's
memory, all of them racing to be the first
to eulogize the sexually ambiguous
singer from the Middle West, sprinting to
see who could make up why he meant
more to them than anyone else. Some
said, Fuck Death, and others said,
We're losing all our heroes, while the
worst said, This year can go to hell. Paul
said nothing and wondered why a petite
man born with an ability to dance well
and sing on tune was the only good
person who ever lived. Why do people
think we could never live without him?
Paul thought that and obsessed over the
narcissistic reactions instead of thinking
of scenes for Mike and Tyler. The way
he shaved his entire head, Mike looked
like an overweight turtle taken out of its
shell. He kept a clean-shaven face,
while Tyler left his hair short on the
sides. Somewhere in the ether Tyler
gyrated his hips like Elvis, his prick
boned-up, as Tyler would say, ready to
spear a co-resident in an unused room
in the hospital. Mike programmed on a
couch in the suburbs of Minneapolis, in
the Southtown area made famous by a
band from Edina that later moved to
Brooklyn. Half-formed, Mike almost
looked like a sculpture abandoned
halfway through, or like a drawing an

animator hadn't bothered coloring. All the while, problems circled in Paul's head. His lady was gone. Throughout their two years she had mentioned other men being handsome, and every time Paul met one or saw one online, the man had hair. The whistling again. Paul grated his teeth and tasted the enamel. He had accomplished nothing that late afternoon besides getting mad at people for being so insecure they had to convince strangers they loved a singer who had past the most.

Entertainer might have been a better word, but there were no more words for Paul. An itch overtook his brain. He opened the folder containing the digital representations of his lady's wanting. Guilt did not flood the erogenous path so badly that he couldn't will himself to rigidity, and soon enough he finished on the wood floor, where his love lay in a pearlescent pool.

—

The wind has stopped blowing, Paul wrote. What kind of opening is that? He continued. May as well write It was a dark and stormy night. Writing about the wind, Paul at least knew, was for bearded adjuncts trying to sound poetic.

A way of taking up time, a cheap way to give a character depth when the only depth was the wind blowing through their hair. Paul had almost none. On top of that, a file on his computer wouldn't delete on that first morning of the weekend. Paul wondered if the developers had programmed the operating system in a way that ensured they, the creators, would live on. No matter how bad their work, they would exist in perpetuity. Paul could relate. After moving around the country and accomplishing nothing he had released two self-published books of autobiographical fiction, replete with typos that no one could say didn't exist. Almost like they existed too much, like the program Paul spent that morning trying to delete. He searched for the solution on his phone, restarting his computer with increased exasperation. Jesus Christ, he whispered, and later, when he was sure he'd found the solution but had not, What the fuck. He longer believed it a sin to swear.

Paul wrestled with the tool needed to construct a story on the problem of being a balding man in the year 2019. Above him he could hear the footsteps of the neighbor his lady had complained to their landlord about, the one who stomped around in heels in the early mornings and on weekends. Paul agreed with the complaint, though secretly he had been worried; once, in the middle of the night, they heard their female neighbor in the midst of passion, and Paul fretted that his lady's complaint would dissuade her from being so vigorous again. Paul's lady had been discontent with the clomping of the heels and with most aspects of the life she and her man had forged. Where she might have gone, Paul could not guess. Back to live with her parents in Dallas? Or to all the places Paul could never take her, like Bora Bora and Seychelles? Paul did not like flying. Like his dad he preferred to drive, and he did not make much money. She could have found another, Paul painfully allowed while restarting his computer again. He was nearly bald and very hungry as the sun started to shine on the brick building across the garden, separated by a wooden fence and short spruce trees. The wind died and picked up intermittently as Paul gave up on deleting the file while Tyler attended a conference for radiologists in a convention hall in D.C.. He passively watched PowerPoint presentations on how to distinguish between the subtle colorations in the brain but really Tyler concentrated on the naked forms being sent to his phone. None among the

senders would be his wife, content at
home with their new baby. Tyler told
confidants she pretty much agreed with
the setup, and as he drank a scotch at
the hotel bar after the presentation, the
bartender couldn't help but notice how
glued to his phone he was, this bald
man who looked like a swimmer but said
he was a radiologist. He hardly looked
up for more than a second to pay before
going up to his room to take a picture of
his growing prick. He had been sent a
video of an Asian-American graduate
student he'd met at a bar in Lincoln
Square. She made choking noises while
swallowing on a dildo and said, in
between spitting up, It's still not as big
as yours. The buzzing of her vibrator
could be heard as Tyler took long
strides down the quiet hallway. The next
morning Mike coded in the North Loop,
in an office not far from the all-night
dance party Minneapolis threw for itself
after the singer Crown passed away.
Mike, bald and increasingly portly, did
not attend the self-congratulatory wake,
nor did he share a story online about the
time he waited in line behind the famous
entertainer at Cub Foods in White Bear
Lake. He'd gone to bed early, as he
always did, and risen early to get back
to the business of being a man who
owned a company. He wore dark-
washed jeans, faded on the thighs, a

purple-collared shirt with French cuffs, and black dress shoes with a long tip, bought on sale at Nordstrom Rack. His mind a complete blank, other than the lines of code.

This is bad, Paul thought, looking at a paragraph of background for his two main characters. After wrestling with an obstinate computer and thinking about the wind and two imaginary bald men who would never be characters that tenured professors lectured on, Paul wanted a change of pace, like a fight involving cheese. He wanted that over the unsolvable problems hovering over him, like balding and stubborn technology and the failure to be something more than someone who lived alone and worked in a cubicle and was balding. He and his lady had fought around macaroni and cheese and cheese fries and cheese curds and gourmet cheeses from the co-op. In Wisconsin, they couldn't avoid fights without cheese somewhere nearby, and Paul pined for that, an argument accompanied by cheese. How much more compelling that would be, he thought, than self-published autobiographical fiction about the melancholy of a balding man. Grinding his teeth once again, Paul loathed everything, knowing he had bothered to record a thought about a thought.

—

After another day entering data Paul could not stop thinking about the weather. On the way to the bathroom, the consistent splashing against rocks in the garden brought him to the time before he met his lady who left, to a date with someone he had messaged online. She worked in advertising and they met at a bar in Uptown, in Minneapolis. They sat across from each other, and when she spoke passionately or laughed loudly she moved her body enough that Paul could see the sweat stains around her armpits. She talked about her work, and Paul was equally boring, as they ate antipasti and drank organic beers, like a stock photo of a first date. That was long ago, and for the whole evening Paul had wanted to get back to writing his novel about balding— this is how far back his desire goes—but he didn't have the brash man sense, like a Mike or a Tyler, to say to the woman, This just isn't going to work, honey, then politely as he could get up and leave. From the restaurant Paul saw across the street a yellow crane, used for the construction of a high-rise condo.

JEFFREY ELLINGER

Moments later the rains came like sheets and the electricity flashed and died and the staff instructed the daters to move away from the window. Paul looked out and could no longer see the crane. His date clung to him. She wore her hair like a supporting actress from a sitcom in the nineties, straight with a curl at the bottom, and she spoke in a muffled voice. She laughed at everything he said, even if it wasn't funny. When the winds died and the rain became more like a drizzle, Paul paid for the meal. At the first residential street they saw a tree on top of a car, splitting it nearly in two. The storm had lifted the tall thick plant out of its foundation the way someone might pull a weed from the ground. On the humid walk to her place they encountered citizens emerging from their homes to survey the damage. They saw downed power lines and heard police sirens. The city pulsed like it does after a disaster. That catastrophic energy spilled over to her entryway, where she showed Paul the floor, which must have been built by Nazis in the sixties. She flipped up the rug and pointed to the swastikas on the tiles. In her apartment they lit candles and she put a movie on her laptop. On the couch she started with her mouth, and later they moved to her damp bed, where she rode Paul like a doctor defibrillating an unconscious patient. The galvanism of the storm caused her to call out his name, and every night for the next week she texted him, but he kept giving excuses, until eventually she stopped.

I have been mean, Paul thought as sirens wailed in Wisconsin, recalling the storm that knocked down trees in Minneapolis years before. I have been heartless and cold, he groused to himself. Like Mike, Paul thought, who proudly told his friends he had never been broken up with. Once Mike came close, as he told his best bros, but he continued to pursue the girl and she didn't break up with him, so he could now happily say he had kept his streak alive. She was the one Mike was with now, and the reason he had not given up was her prodigious physical endowment. She was a zealous believer in God, but before Mike started seeing her he had spent the previous ten years of his life deriding anyone who espoused a fundamental belief in Jesus Christ. I am heartless like Tyler, Paul thought: Tyler, who plunged his member down the bartender's throat after she had come up to his room on the last night of his radiology conference. Tyler's wife, who stayed at home with their baby, thought it all a big game, the way

JEFFREY ELLINGER

Tyler would point out college students at
the beach and brazenly like pictures of a
blonde co-resident on social media.
Closer to bald every day, Paul could
look back in time and see the
transgressions and add them up. Unlike
Tyler or Mike, who never thought
anything could be a sin, Paul could see
why the universe needed him to be bald,
to balance the cruelty, the selfishness.

What is this? Paul thought. He had read
The Lost Weekend over the last
weekend, and though Paul did not drink
to the point of dependency he did
obsessively crave validation as a man
who wrote for a living, going to extreme
deluded lengths, like his own "In a
Glass." How awful would that be, Paul
thought, sitting at his peeling desk from
the Martha Stewart Collection, to write
about how I am writing a novel about a
guy who wrote a novel about a guy who
never wrote a novel because he wasn't
a writer but an alcoholic who only cared
about where his next drink came from.
Paul's lady had left, and his prospects
as he approached the age at which
society starts calling you over the hill did
not strike him as appealing. The week
before, Paul had applied for another job
at the social services company where
he entered data, and after he turned in
his résumé to the other department his

immediate supervisor reminisced with
him. I told you the story, right? she said,
taking a mirror out of her purse and
folding it on her desk to put on more
makeup. Her florid perfume gave Paul a
headache. Like when you applied, she
said. I told everyone in the office, this
guy is so random, but I'm going to
interview him anyway.

As if the craziest thing that had ever
happened, Paul thought, shielded from
the storm outside, was for someone with
experience as a Data Supporter,
Packager, Dispatcher, Loader, Shear
Operator, Houseparent, Child Care
Counselor, In-School Suspension
Supervisor, Boat Waxer, and Freelance
Writer to apply for a job posted on
Craigslist that tasked the applicant with
driving into the poorest areas of a dying
city to interview destitute families and
after that write reports on whether or not
those families should be awarded
money for taking care of a relative's
child. Not a job anyone would want, so it
seemed to Paul logical enough that he
would end up working alongside people
with similar job histories, in data support
and in packaging and dispatching and
loading and shearing and
houseparenting and in-school
suspension supervising and boat waxing
and freelance writing.

JEFFREY ELLINGER

Paul sat at his wobbly desk, wanting his lady to come back. She knew that a hair on his cheek between his right eye and nose grew back as fast as a mushroom. She knew that he had gas every morning upon waking. She knew how he liked his eggs scrambled and a million other things no one else ever bothered to learn. The thunder cracked. Paul put his hand over his head and felt the rubbery scalp. What had Tyler and Mike done when they found themselves down to so little? Paul wanted to talk to them as the rain came down, to ask their advice, to see what wise words they'd have in his time of need to guide him through. There was only the sound of weather.

—

Paul lived near the cold great lake in the rusted city but worked in the western suburbs, in a monstrous building near the fairgrounds that once housed a thriving business, back when manufacturing jobs existed in Wisconsin. Those jobs are gone now, and the building is mostly deserted floors interspersed with cubicle farms. Ridiculous, Paul thought, that it would be this cold as he drove to work, but also fortuitous. His car's cooling system had recently flunked, and other parts of his car coughed their last breaths. Paul dreamed of selling the beater and making it as a true and honest writer of autobiographical fiction. But that, he also knew, was the half-cocked pipe dream of a man destined to work at regular jobs while fantasizing about selling his earthly goods and chasing after some half-cocked pipe dream of being a true and honest writer of autobiographical fiction. All Paul did when he got home was stare at his phone, masturbate, and dream.

My lady has left me, Paul thought, and I am alone. Unlike Apollinaire, Paul had not been wounded in battle. Unlike Jackson, Paul did not write a story about someone who cannot write a story. Paul only became more troubled. Tyler did not worry about his baldness. Graduate students in Logan Square sent him pictures after trips to salons where they were denuded except for a strategic triangle. Mike, on the other hand, did not desire naked millennials in the prime of their vibrancy. All he wanted was for his tech company to make millions so he could cash in on the spite he had accumulated over years of working with, as he called them, Silicon Valley douchebag fuck-sticks, and anyone else he ever met who made him petition for money. In Mike's heaven, founders came to his home in the southern suburbs of Minneapolis and took turns licking the bottom of his boot as they cried for one tiny ounce of lube while Mike pushed a rod into them in his garage stuffed with tools he never used for do-it-yourself projects he never finished. Retribution for the times they made Mike grovel or be less than the Mike he wanted to be. Balding had nothing to do with anything other than genetics, Mike knew, and his lack of hair did not affect his power. At the height of his faith, in college, Mike religiously studied Ayn Rand, and though he had since disavowed any philosophical associations with the objectivist and become a staunch liberal, Mike still, in his heart of hearts, respected only those who contributed value. Everyone who didn't was, as he said in private, a leech or a dummy or both. Mike never repeated these truisms on his social media accounts. Instead, he retweeted leading progressive thinkers. Mike coded while Tyler, at a hotel room for a radiology conference, video-chatted with his wife in Charleston. She babbled on as Tyler absently looked over at his phone. When asked, Tyler would say Paul had texted, but really Tyler gawked at fresh breasts. Another ding, and a

picture of a round ass with a tail coming
out of it.

Balding, what does it mean, Paul wrote.
Then he got up to use the bathroom.
Upon returning to his deteriorating desk
Paul saw what he had written and
almost threw up, then almost threw up
again for thinking he would throw up for
thinking something so trite, and on it
went like that until his brain interrupted
him with the memory of his lady, who
was gone.

Cold outside, Paul wrote. How much
longer will it stay this way. Maybe
forever. A permanent freeze. Jake
Gyllenhaal.

Paul wrote all that and, with not a single
hair like a movie star's, worried over
why his lady had left. Not because of
how badly he gave love or how little he
meant at his job or how few elegant
nights his salary could afford—no, he
feared, she had left him for being bald.
Paul hoped, as he had almost every day
of his adult life, to wake one morning
and find that the tides had turned and
God again loved him like when he was a
baby. Pure out of the womb, with no
imperfections just a head full of angelic
blond locks, everyone would want the

very best for him. When that day came all baldness would reverse, and Paul dreamed he'd find himself with more hair than he used to have, like when famous athletes reemerge into the spotlight after a season away. In May it was cold. Paul had done nothing of substance. Hungry again, he knew if he ate he would get comfortable and want to play his video games or stare at his phone, and after that he'd become sleepy, and once he got sleepy he would not want to do a thing, and the thought bubbles about how he really should get something done would pop before they ever inflated, and he'd get ready for bed. Once he fell into slumber, the next day would come.

Colder than the day before, and grayer, too, like the city had reached an undiscovered shade within the Pantone system. Here it is, Paul wrote, the grayest day in history. But I've got to keep going, he thought. I've got to make something worthless that no one will ever see.

Full of pathetic self-defeating thoughts in the apartment after work, Paul found himself at the Baseball Reference page for Scott Leius, who in the 1990s played third base for the Minnesota Twins.

Looking up what Leius did now, Paul learned the former major leaguer coached baseball at a camp in New York. If Scott Leius had been born ten years later, Paul hypothesized, he could have played in a time of astronomical salaries and would never have had to coach at small-time camps in New York. Scott Leius could go on trips to Las Vegas or the Bahamas or wherever retired wealthy sportsmen go to wear heavy colognes and dress in loose-fitting slacks and Hawaiian shirts and smoke cigars. At his self-constructed desk from the Martha Stewart Collection, Paul kept getting distracted with puerile thoughts like what Scott Leius did after retirement. Those kinds of distractions made it harder for Paul to start a work of autobiographical fiction that showed and did not tell and also did not use the word "cement" when Paul meant concrete and did not describe every other room one of the characters stood in as being built with cement and even more crucially did not use the word "cement" at all. So far, Paul's story amounted to a guy in a room bemoaning his past and agonizing over his future, like some modern version of Bernhard's *Concrete*, except much more obscure.

It is not a non sequitur to say now that Paul's lady was full of sorrow and Paul could never figure out why. Born as a Cancer, he said a feminine moon ruled him, but he did not understand. On the couch after work, their joint supper finished, they would have nothing to do but tell jokes and look at pictures of strangers in yoga poses in Tulum and plan weekend getaways and covet all they wanted to buy at online boutiques. They would do that, but at some point after putting away the dishes he would see her face contort and know that soon he would be trying to console her. Sometimes she cried so much Paul did not think her body could produce more water. Sometimes he'd kiss her face in the morning and taste dried salt. Sometimes he'd just sit there and be mesmerized by the human body's capacity for sadness. For his part, Paul never cried. Many times he wanted to, hoping that might jolt her back, but he could never muster the tears, no matter how hard he tried to push them out of his body.

She cried so much because I was bald, Paul thought. I was balding and she could do nothing to stop the dying. A Ben Nino song played in Paul's headphones. Ben Nino had been bald for some time, Paul thought, but no one talked about that. It could be argued, Paul continued to think, that Nino's baldness added a layer of mystical fog, enabling the British songwriter to release record after record that tricked listeners into believing it was not the same note but a series of collapsing stars only someone as bald as Ben Nino could interpret for the common man. Paul turned off the music and began to watch hippies in Texas giving and receiving massages while speaking in soft tones. They showed off their large backsides in tight black stretch pants, and sometimes their ample breasts pushed out to the sides as they lay facedown on the massage table. Paul drifted away from the apartment along the cold lake and pretended he had become the Svengali who brainwashed hippies into staying at a farm outside Austin with decorative throw pillows and bottles of lotions and a pool out back, where everyone wore a bikini and helped each other keep their thick thighs loosened. Blocks away, Paul's car sat parked. How often had Paul's lady become upset over never having any parking. In Milwaukee of all places, she would say, and Paul had to grin at how crazy it was beginning to make him as well, to have no parking and to know how prescient his lady had been. Their landlord once assured them there would be plenty of parking, but that was a lie, like everything else. Paul turned off his computer and headed to the bedroom. He switched over to his phone. The stretching enthusiasts had nowhere to go. They lived on organic strawberries and good vibes. They loved unconditionally.

—

The next night Paul got drunk and went on social media, where he posted two pictures of himself. If his lady still lived in the apartment, Paul knew, he would have saved himself the embarrassment. He would not have wanted to risk staying up late to attempt to gain traction online because he knew that would go nowhere, and when he'd gotten nowhere he would still have to go in and wake her up with his lumbering body crashing into bed. They would have gotten into an argument and he might have ended up on the couch, and there he would not sleep, a song looping in his head, until at some point in the middle of the night exhaustion took over. The pictures Paul posted were dark, not full of libidinal light, the opposite of the ones he liked featuring athletic yoga instructors doing splits in thongs on the beaches of Bali. Paul had thought his posts could be appealing, but the next morning with no hearts he saw them as they were: unpolished, like the selfies of a straight white bald bearded guy who wore camouflage and played *Call of Duty* in his parents' basement as he drank Mountain Dew and posted on Reddit and said the biggest thrill of his life was going on an African safari and killing a leopard from a Jeep with a high-powered rifle after drinking foreign beers since 6 a.m.

With a foggy head Paul got up to go to work. The day before he'd said something and he was in guilt. Paul could not get a distracting cycle out of his head until a new one budged in, this time about a client who'd hit on a coworker in the elevator. Clients in the building where Paul worked sought life skills and transitional living services, along with therapy and medication management. One of them, his coworker had told him, approached her and said she was a pretty young lady. The man was developmentally delayed, and Paul mentioned—after the coworker approximated the man's age at around forty—that the guy must be at the height of his powers. He'd said that even though he knew he would later be in guilt. He knew he was not cut out for making light of anything, yet he did it anyway, as if his mind had a mind of its own.

JEFFREY ELLINGER

Free will is a farce, Paul thought at his cubicle. His head pounding, his beard a mess, his clothes frumpy, his shirt untucked, his hair almost gone. What are Tyler and Mike doing, Paul thought, but that thought soon was replaced with the pressing weight of mind-numbing data entry. Paul took a drink from his cold-pressed coffee, swishing the liquid around in his mouth. Momentarily the irrigation cleared the muddy path, but soon files piled up, brought by an administrative assistant who quietly said, Peep, so as to mark her hushed arrival. She made Paul jump that day, as she did every day, and as she left Paul wished he had never thought drinking could act as a motivator to get his autobiographical novel about balding off the ground. It lay like a dead animal, or like one that never developed out of the evolutionary chain and now is not even in the extinct portion of science books.

Tyler and Mike, Paul thought as he rubbed his temples in the cubicle, what are they doing? Paul could sit there all day and do nothing and knew that no one would notice. He browsed for soft music. Even if the workers in the cube farm were technically prohibited from

using streaming websites, it was critical,
seemingly a mortal issue, to wear
headphones to drown out the other
conversations. Tyler and Mike worked,
Paul wrote in an email to himself, but
their baldness did not inhibit their
production. Tyler, a radiologist, helped
his wife with their baby over the
weekends by taking the infant out to his
garage, where he was rebuilding a Jeep
from scratch, and where he opened
acres of sexts. If Tyler ever got a
hangover, he joked about it, saying with
a wry smile, Oh fuck we partied last
night. Houses and children and Jeeps
and fields of weed and ripe asses with
dildos sliding in and out all filmed from
behind by a girl attending Northwestern
for religious studies who once gave
Tyler the best blow job he ever had, as
he told his Brazilian surrogate brother
who'd lived in Tyler's parents' house in
high school. Mike, bald like a baby
plucked out of the womb too soon, sat in
a North Loop office across the street
from which was the oldest restaurant in
Minneapolis. Nearby was a store run by
the sons of the fathers of the Target
Corporation where they sold denim
jeans for $250 a pair. Mike coded on a
laptop in a cavernous space in a brick
building that once produced chocolate in
the nineteenth century. He could rub his
bald head and not think twice. Bad

things happened to people who didn't make good things happen, Mike said, and the two coders he'd hired the month before looked up. They did not question their boss and returned to their laptops. Mike continued to look forward. He did not believe in cosmic forces, only the worth he could produce by adding to the database. He got back to coding.

I am so worthless, Paul thought as he peed into the urinal at work, shooting yellow out of his flaccid member. Other than his baldness, which he could see in the mirror in the bright light of the bathroom, it was his double chin and the dark circles under his eyes and his average lovemaking, he knew, that had made his lady leave him. She had gone to find a better everything. Paul threw away the paper towel and went back to his cubicle, where the last hairs on his head did not provide comfort. Unproductivity assailed him once more.

—

On another day after data entry getting up from the couch and stopping his watch was an option, but, Paul knew, if he did that, he'd have to start all over pumping himself up to get to the edge of writing about balding again. Paul also

had to get his mind off of his lady
leaving him, and somehow forget about
his sagging double chin and the dark
circles under his eyes and the fat
around his middle, his ever decreasing
amount of hair. The overhead fan
cooled the first-floor apartment. Paul
wanted to turn it down, but that would
mean getting up from the couch, and he
was glued. He had not yet turned on his
laptop, which lay on the IKEA coffee
table she'd left behind. What a dead
weight, the writing machine, Paul
thought. Why should I open it? The sun
might one day desiccate all human
accomplishment. What's the point? On
his phone Paul researched and found
that science was toying with the idea of
using an asteroid to offset the world's
rotational path. Only vanity, Paul
thought; we could wake up tomorrow
and be blotted out by space debris.

We drive around in our cars and say
words to each other and really think
we're doing something, Paul thought on
the couch. He stopped thinking and
scrolled through his phone. The device
immobilized him, as though an invisible
tether attached them. He could sit like
that for a good while, clicking deeper,
until he found himself no longer a
person. As though he'd taken a
hallucinogen, he became one with the

device, and the universe melted. The ticking of his watch. The whirr of the ceiling fan. Consistent sounds acted as reminders of doing nothing. Paul could not afford a better watch, one with a quieter mechanism, that looked as stylish. It was one of those things that were just out of reach, as if the world's companies had convened at some point in history and decided to include a crucial deficiency in every affordable product in order to make people generally unsatisfied with their lives, so they worked harder to tear others down so that they could achieve a better station in which they were the ones who could afford the subdued watch with the lower decibels, the alternative being to tolerate life with the cheaper timepiece and hope one day their luck turns or the watch wears down enough that it stops ticking so loud.

That will not be for years, Paul thought, a good twenty minutes into watching videos of a woman in her forties trying on clothes from a wardrobe subscription service. She dyed her hair black, lived in a sterile condo with framed drab art on her white walls, and ranted about the stylist who picked out her clothes. She just isn't getting me, the woman said of the stylist, and with each outfit the yearning woman chose at least one

thing wrong, as if the baby stylist in
West Hollywood had more than maybe
five minutes to throw together the
blouses and shoes and have them sent
to San Diego, where the woman
perhaps dreamed of one day attracting
a man to take her to salsa classes.

Paul protected himself from the winds
shooting out of the ceiling fan by putting
his arms inside his shirt. Blades
whipped the air. When he'd first walked
in—hot and sweaty from the three-block
walk from his car to the front door—the
setting had been right. Another twenty
minutes and Paul found himself
watching videos of a young woman
unboxing clothes from a different
subscription service. Paul fast-
forwarded to the part where, judging
from the preview, he thought she might
complete a turn in her leggings, and she
did, and she had so much backside.
Very pale, she wore no makeup, and
Paul watched five more of her videos to
see her form from other angles. There
were thousands of others on the
internet, but Paul focused on hers. She
could be his next wife, he thought, until
she mentioned a daughter, and he
clicked away, knowing he could never
provide enough. Also, even in his fat
bald state, Paul thought himself too
good, that he could find someone with

less baggage. He did not want someone with a child or the woman complaining in her condo. He wanted a fantasy. The watch ticked. The fan blew, and Paul became sleepy, like he could never get enough sleep, like he could hibernate. No one expected anything of him.

No one is expecting anything of me, Paul thought as he drifted off. The ticking and the fan kept him out of a deep restfulness, so he flipped between consciousness and unconsciousness, aware of doing nothing but not cogent enough to do anything about it, like in the morning after a long sleep and you want to make a tight fist and you try with all your might, but your grip is as strong as a baby's.

—

Out of nowhere Paul's balls teemed with electricity, as if pads connected to his scrotum pulsated energy through his sack to his spermatic cord, like a live wire cut down in a storm. Another day of data entry. Paul knew he had nothing to look forward to, and his balls being electric did not count. The autobiographical novel on balding would take years, and it would take more years to find an agent, and more years after that to be published. His job, going nowhere. He keyed in data all day. The position related to nothing he loved: eating pho, women with big butts and thick thighs wearing yoga pants in used bookstores, complaining about his life. Paul had not grown up with screenwriter parents in Bel Air. Paul's parents worked as a schoolteacher and a beef cattle farmer in South Dakota. His graduating public school class in a rural part of the Middle West comprised twenty-six students, and he was never groomed for a profession. As a boy, Paul wanted to be baseball player. As a teen, a professional golfer. In early adulthood he thought he would be a missionary. After he apostatized Paul found himself working where a person with unrealistic goals ends up: hard labor, driving around delivering goods, then data entry. Paul once told his mom, when she asked what he wanted to do when he grew up—and this was after hedging and bumbling for a while in the backseat of the family car—I want to help people.

I hate what I have become, Paul thought, over thirty years later. Morosely, Paul toyed with tweeting just that, I hate what I have become, but he could not bring himself to open the app, and that made him more depressed, that he had thought of a way to stay relevant but could not bring himself to go through with sending the relevance out into the world.

So Paul went to rest—Mike and Tyler stayed inert, not coding or sexting—and there in the bed he once shared with his lady Paul's mind drifted off to those he could weave into his autobiographical novel on the plight of the balding man, those from his past who could be used as fiber. Lindsey the redhead, Sara the blonde, and Emily the petite. They joined him after taking mushrooms at a Dave Matthews concert in Portland. The three women worked for the same nonprofit company he delivered to—this was back when he had more hair—and somewhere during "Two Step" they drifted away, doing that shoulder-swaying dance. By the time they found a quiet space they were rolling. In a forest off the grounds of the festival—bushes in the backyard of a large house—-they undressed and talked to the leaves before Lindsey, the self-proclaimed make-out queen, began kissing Paul. The petite one, Emily, saw this and took Sara, the blonde, and began kissing her neck. Soon enough they were mixed in an unorganized but seeking pile. In the morning they woke to leaves pasted over them like an organic decoupage, crusted with Paul's seed. That night would be the wildest night Paul ever experienced, and he pointed to his hair as the problem now, since not long after that night the four of them stopped going to as many jam band concerts. Time went along and Paul met Elise. He lost more hair and quit that job. He got married and later divorced.

There isn't much to say anymore, Paul thought, unable to sleep. He could not bring himself to look at his phone. Crown is dead from a drug overdose. The whole country has forgotten about the genocide of its first people. Like one of those swirls of garbage in the ocean, Paul's thoughts became a cesspool circling a drain. He thought of tweeting: My thoughts are a cesspool circling a drain never to be unplugged lol. He even composed the draft before giving in and tossing his phone across the bed, where it teetered at the edge only to drop to the floorboards with a cracking sound. Paul crawled across the bed and looked over the edge, and saw the device lying on its screen. He could not bear to flip the phone over and see if he had injured his closest friend and worst enemy, the thing he looked to to tell him he had moved up in the world but that always greeted him with coldness, never blinking with notifications that his self-

published short stories had been
uncovered and would now be published
by *Bamfa* in an issue devoted to
unheralded artists.

Where is she, Paul thought, not daring
to look at his phone. Outside the
apartment, worms came up out of the
ground through the cracks in the
sidewalk. Unknowingly they embarked
on a suicide mission. Once Paul had
been sensitive enough that he would try
to save them by tossing them back in
the moist earth. Wind blew outside. The
invisible wind, rattling the old windows.
Black Elk talked of the wind beautifully,
Paul thought. Somewhere else outside a
man was caught sneaking into the
bedrooms of single women. The violator
stood there and watched those poor
women sleep until they woke to a
stranger at the side of their bed.
Thousands of miles away, Paul's lady
hiked in Italy. Up in the atmosphere, a
tiny rock collided with the moon. The
tides in Kauai receded slightly.

—

Done with another day of data entry,
Paul tried on clothes from a subscription
box. After years of heavy lifting at
manual labor jobs and never running—

he claimed his shins hurt and his calves tightened to the point where the circulation to his feet cut off and he couldn't breathe after four hundred meters—he found he had developed boobs. The lightweight shirts from the trunk he'd ordered online—one of his lady's last suggestions for sprucing up his wardrobe—showcased his nipples, so that he felt like a teenage girl pleading for attention. In the promotional email the outfits looked great, sorted by a millennial in Portland, who, he imagined, must go to Coachella in tops that would not contain his new boobs. Dejected, Paul stopped trying after the third shirt, foreseeing the results if he tried on every garment. They'd sent the biggest shirts they carried, even one marked XXL.

I need to shop at a big-and-tall store, Paul said to no one. He stuck out his gut and turned in the full-length mirror to emphasize how silly it was that he had signed up for a service meant for fitter men. This is a humiliation service, he said out loud. With no one else around, Paul's words yielded no reply. Clothes scattered on the floor of a bedroom close to empty without his lady's things: perfumes and jewelry and baskets of sweaters. She left over an evening, with every trip taking more of her. They did not speak. He drank and played his baseball video game while she marched back and forth, her jaw clenched.

Paul looked in the mirror. His lady had warned him about lifting weights and not doing cardio. You'll get bigger tits than me, she half joked. She had large breasts and stubby legs, thick and flexible. She taught yoga on weekends. She might be in Costa Rica, Paul thought, but he did not know. He stood staring at the wide mass he had evolved into, and the vision staring back left him in peculiar awe. In high school Paul wanted to be bigger and stronger, to have a manly body. Now he wished he could switch back to the lanky, thin-waisted boy, all arms and legs, with a jutting chin cutting the air. How like me, Paul thought, to get the thing I once wanted at a time when I don't need it.

Mike and Tyler never stared at themselves in mirrors. Tyler, built like a swimmer, could eat pounds of noodles and feet of sandwiches and boxes of pizza and drink gallons of Scotch and beer and not gain a pound. He could throw on any clean t-shirt before going out—and they all slipped on no problem—and take one girl out for dinner and get her to pay for appetizers and drinks, then go to her place for everything rapturous and leave before midnight, saying he needed to work in the morning, then go out for late-night bar food with another and end up at hers, almost in the morning, where they'd get high and she'd make pancakes and have Tyler eat her with syrup drizzled over her shapely ass, and still he would not gain an ounce. Bald and lithe, like a sailor who worked on a wooden schooner in the 1700s, whaling for precious oil.

Mike, rotund like Paul, did not go one day without loving himself. Even when he lost all his hair before the end of college, Mike's confidence never wavered. To compensate, in his late twenties Mike put on eyeliner before going to a club, or he played acoustic guitar at a house party, or he started a website, or he came up with the definition of a word when no one else could. Now obese by medical standards, and bald for over fifteen years, Mike never looked in his full-length bedroom mirror to think anything other than *I look great*. Photogenic, with a natural smile in any picture of any assembled group, Mike could stand tall next to elementary school teachers or antisocial coders or friends at the bar on Eat Street and know he was strong—Mike never lost any of the physical fights he got into with other guys—and he was smart. In medieval times, portliness was considered a sign of opulence, Paul imagined Mike saying, and Mike would be right, and Mike would know Mike was right while living in Minneapolis, not Silicon Valley, as Mike believed himself to be above the mob. Tyler lived in the South with his wife and their chubby blonde child who would never know the extent to which her father had been with other women, or, if she did, it would not be until much later, when she realized she had destructive habits; and when she went to her mother to ask what it was like when they were young, her mom would say, It's time for you to learn the truth about your father.

As Paul formed these thoughts, Tyler and Mike started to seem real. Almost as real as Paul, who continued to stare at himself in the mirror, or the himself he assumed must be his physical representation. It was not a close facsimile, he thought: as though a caricature artist had been paid to inflate the worst of him, or a mad sculptor with syphilis working around the time of the Renaissance—or, Paul wondered, would it be during the Reformation? Did they happen at the same time? Paul did not know. He had long abandoned the hope of ever trying to remember anything.

Sculptor, Paul thought, as the sunlight dimmed. The bedroom became darker. (Paul could not bear the scrutiny of overhead light. His lady had taken the lamp and he had not bought another.) Everybody respects a sculptor, Paul thought, the manliest artist there is.

For a second, almost even smiling, Paul knew Mike would be able to think of a better answer for the manliest artist. Seeing the fat around his armpits, Paul stopped. Mike was not real, and how stupid it was to think about what a fictional person would say. The self-reproach did not bode well for someone who wanted everyone in the world to call him a great composer of elegant prose in made-up stories. Regardless, Paul did not do anything that night, like many others.

—

Paul stared at the computer screen in his cubicle on another day or month or year. According to a quiz advertising an experimental movie by a Greek director, Paul would be a duck. A slick-feathered, half-fish half-bird, with a member so small it could not be seen outside of a laboratory: that's what Paul would be. Switching from the online quiz, Paul watched an outsider musician talking about the videos he liked most on the internet, one after another, grainy, fetishistic fare: men smoking cigars or fixing their Wranglers; men walking through muddy fields in skimpy underwear; a man in a suit slipping into a bathtub full of water. The troublemaker musician slyly said he liked that one because it was his way of living out a fantasy, since, he said, he would never work in a cubicle.

A shiver went down Paul's spine. He worked in a cubicle, and he would continue to work in a cubicle, maybe for the rest of his life. Living in discordance with an imagined reality, Paul did not waver from his belief that he could be more than what he was, that he could be like the musician, as famous and capable of snappy remarks. Instead of writing songs, Paul thought, he could write autobiographical novels no one read and subsist on grants.

The phone rang, breaking the fantasy. Then another. The big mamas in the other cubicles never answered on the second ring. A third ring, and the light on Paul's phone's housing unit blinked, waiting for a response. Paul tensed, as if on a dirt-packed road in a town in the Old West. The big mamas stood yards away, their fingers resting near the triggers of their pink six-shooters. Who had the big balls? Beginning of the fourth ring, and the showdown reached its climax. Any more rings and their boss could come out. Phone's ringing, she would say pointedly, anyone going to answer it?

The history of antebellum America. The heroic movement for civil rights. Black Lives Matter. Ku Klux Klan. Names like Paul Duke, Rodney King, and Freddie Gray. Richard Spencer. Trayvon Martin. All the problems of being white in America and being black in America swirled between them, and at the last possible instant each picked up their receiver and spoke, and each heard the dial tone. The Latina administrative assistant, stationed in the front, had picked up. Staggered clicks and the terse faceoff was finished, until the next time. The showdown could have been called a normal occurrence, and for Paul it exemplified why he coveted the musician's life, his laissez-faire allusions to the effect that he would never stoop so low as to be a drone in a cubicle. The Canadian musician, who admired Jonathan Richman just as Paul did,

could watch videos of middle-aged men
at the end of their ropes relieving the
metaphysical stress of their everyday
lives by dipping themselves, fully
clothed, into bathtubs of water, all the
while obscuring their faces because
they knew, at the end of the day, they
needed their soul-draining office job.

Not even lunchtime, and Paul was
hungry again. The constant desire for
food he saw as a problem, along with
the balding, and also his lady being
gone. Those were constants, axiomatic
to existence, that he would want to eat
and be bald and that his lady would
leave him. The working in the cubicle
where he entered data could be
changed, Paul believed somehow.
Being chained there did not have to be a
lifetime sentence. Nothing was
predetermined at birth, he hoped. His
work computer threatened to autoplay
the next video. Outside the cube Paul
could hear one of his coworkers on her
cell phone, laughing a laugh that
sounded like she would choke from not
breathing. He could not see her or any
of the others but knew what they'd be
doing, scrolling through text messages
from the time when they lived with their
husbands, who had left like Paul's lady
had left. Maybe they were looking at
saucy pictures of shirtless men, or

reading an article linked from social media. The most recent one circulating posited that all Chinese food was made of rat meat. I wonder, Paul thought, as he turned on ambient music and grabbed another file, would a duck and a rat even get along?

—

In his mind Paul listed the things to worry about for the weekend: if his boots could be repaired or if he had put off resoling them for too long, causing them to be irreparably threadbare; his lack of hair; the number of garments in his wardrobe in need of alteration; if he should sell his car or put another quarter in the capitalist pinball machine and trade it in for another; if he should apply for yet another job at the social services company or unplug entirely and hike the Ice Age Trail. Far fewer books circulated about that trail than about the Pacific Coast or the Appalachian, with their inspirational tales about how after years of sex and drugs the main character decides they need to get clean and commune with nature so as to be the whitest person who has ever lived in the history of time. White people are from another planet, Paul thought, and regretted the thought immediately,

knowing how tired it was. On a Friday
evening there was nowhere to go. So
Paul went online, to the store that was
eating up all the other stores, and
purchased a collection of poems called
Just before the Divorce. The title would
have seemed prophetic, had Paul
bought the collection before his wife or
lady left, but now it seemed more like
catching up, like trends in fashion, the
right car to buy, the right city to live in.
The author of the collection, mostly
unknown now, had been known as an
author when he lived. At least he had
that much, Paul thought, on the couch in
the quiet apartment. People read his
work and publishers waited on his
pages. Editors fretted they might not do
a good enough job with his words.

Paul had no plans for the weekend other
than worrying: about his small number
of social media followers, the way he
had parked his car, his lack of hair, how
bad he was at networking with Important
Creatives online. The literature scene,
Paul believed, was a sewer of human
ambition that he wanted to be a piece of
feces within, floating not even near the
top. At the bottom would be fine, he
thought, and was sure that if he wrote
as much as bald Mike coded, he would
have become a minor player, the kind of
guy who spoke at book conferences,

taught at a decent university, planned his year around the AWP Conference, and on occasion bedded nice-looking creative writing graduate students. Mike's persistence, his heartless selfish ambition, his blind will, kept him at his keyboard.

If I had that kind of willpower, Paul thought, I could be someone. Like the guy who called himself Captain Fiction once said, I see the notion of talent as quite irrelevant. I see instead perseverance, application, industry, assiduity, will. And that made sense to Paul. As much sense as when Yates said, Plain luck, after all, may be the one thing a good writer needs most. Both pieces of guidance made more sense than the hackneyed advice given by Important Creatives with trust funds whose job, it seemed to Paul, was to post the compliments they received on their social media profiles and in subsequent updates on their self-congratulating timelines use pompous adjectives that screamed insecure to describe their trip to the coffee shop. Something about the inchoate pedestrians and the insouciant barista and their antipodal stance on artificial creamers. The irony being that Paul yearned hard to be like them, to one day be hated by someone just as yearning who had to look up to Paul, whose job, it would seem to the yearner, was to spend most of his day collecting royalties and patting himself on the back.

Tyler never used showy words. He had no need to do so. His knowledge of the human body and its workings sufficed. He could locate nerves and call them by their correct Latin names. The most elaborate words Tyler used outside of work were "smegma," "mons pubis," or anything related to genitalia. And "bang," he liked that one the most. That weekend Tyler played with his dog and worked on his Jeep, his go-cart, and his sailboat. When asked, he posed for pictures with his daughter for his wife's family-oriented social media account. When left alone, Tyler texted, "Wanna bang u" to girls he had known in Chicago. Bald Tyler would be rich, with an upcoming full-time position as an attending radiologist whose specialty Paul—getting out his phone for the inevitable release before bed—did not know, and did not want to know. This only made him more depressed, to see the chasm widening between what he knew and what someone he used to know—back when they lived in the same house in Chicago and vied for the same attention—had learned.

—

Another day, home from the cubicle,
Paul touched the ring finger of his left
hand. When he was married to Elise, he
always played with his ring. Off and on,
on and off, flicking it on a table and
making it spin, even putting the ring in
his mouth. She never cared. In a more
solid marriage, Paul thought, a wife
would be upset that her husband was
always fiddling with the sign of their
attachment. For her part, Elise wore her
ring only some of the time. To work,
intermittently, and as decoration when
they went out, like to a party with her
colleagues or old friends. With no ring,
Paul thought, I need to cut my
fingernails. They had become long
enough that the keratin would be the
first to touch the keys, not the satisfying
flesh. But he did not touch the keys. He
sat on the couch after another day of
data entry, restlessly vacillating between
doing nothing or going back to an extant
hard drive to sift through stories, some
as old as ten years, and all from before
the wedding to Elise .After their union
Paul published two autobiographical
novels—with the last one selling fewer
than ten copies—and when he
publicized that second novel's birth on

JEFFREY ELLINGER

social media the announcement
received a single favorite, along with a
reply from someone he'd met long ago
in Austin, telling him she was engaged.
That whole process so demoralized
Paul that he saved everything on a hard
drive and stacked up the hundreds of
pages and hid them away in a chest.
Now they lay buried under insurance
papers and birthday cards from relatives
who, Paul believed, should have given
up on him, along with romantic
memorabilia from his lady who left:
valentines, movie stubs, plane tickets.

What am I going to do? Paul wondered,
and he did think like this on the couch. A
Monday night like any other: he had no
options. He was so desperate, he
thought of downloading a dating app,
but he stopped short, knowing that he'd
just end up writing melodramatic
autobiographical fiction about finding
and losing love online, full of typos and
grammatical issues, as he had already
done. What made it so bad was how
much hope Paul had had for his first
novel. Its tepid reception—even from
people he once called friends—defeated
him so soundly he halfheartedly
released the second only because he'd
promised himself he would.

There must be something salvageable in there, Paul thought, ruminating on the hard drive in the chest. He did not move from the couch. I wonder if anyone has ever written an entire novel where the main character never goes anywhere other than his own couch. Paul doubted it, though he was not that well-read. It was possible that such a book existed and he wasn't aware of it. Like Knausgaard Himself, Paul believed a great majority of novels were bad. He thought next about tweeting a storm about all fiction being the result of marketing and academia coming together in an unholy marriage, unknowingly engineering a product from a dire formula where one entity is full of itself and out of touch with the human experience and that entity acts as the driving force behind what is considered good while the other receives its cues from the snooty base, thereby pushing stillborn words upon everyone too afraid to criticize because what is published has the support of those who are supposed to be the smartest people in the room but really they are flaccid milk-drinkers on mushrooms.

And neither group has ever felt a real emotion in their whole life, Paul thought on the couch, not typing. The hard drive sat in the trunk. Soil the Natives slept on

179

before the invention of the wheel lay feet
below. The core of the earth burned
lower still. Paul turned on the television.
The yelling of bald men soothed him.
They shouted about the lives of younger
men with hair who hit a ball for a living.
These men whose problems, centered
around maintaining an acceptable
batting average with runners on base,
seemed minuscule to Paul. To have so
much money, Paul thought, how great,
and to also have attractive possibilities
in different cities? And to do something
you loved? There should never be a sad
professional ballplayer, Paul thought.
His worldview, after many tumultuous
intervening years, had not changed
much since boyhood. He got up, made
himself cereal. He ate the cereal and he
masturbated. Later, he fell asleep.

—

Christians love Coldplay, Paul said to no
one in the darkness of the apartment. A
warm rain fell. My throat hurts, he
continued. Almost August and my throat
hurts. I am a piece of garbage who will
rot away and become dust. Paul was
not well. The night before, he'd watched
a special on Wisconsin Public Television
about a man who started a tapas
restaurant, the kind with four dollar signs

in the reviews, where everyone wants to go though no one leaves full, the kind of place where you might feel a little sheepish ordering, as many of the items are foreign, though it all blends together in the end and tastes like butter and bread and meat and cheese and vegetables. The man, who had the same bloated form as Paul, started one of those restaurants and answered when people called him chef. The man was bald, and had been for a while, judging by the lack of coverage on his white scalp and the way he shaved the sides down to nothing. But the man had become something, Paul thought. He'd used the beef from cattle his own father raised and started a small-plates restaurant where beautiful people wanted to dine. Paul's father raised cattle, and Paul wondered whether, if he had used homegrown beef in a restaurant, he would have by now been featured in a public television special on up-and-coming restaurateurs who utilized the untapped resources of South Dakota. Watching the Wisconsin Public Television host use words like haute-casual to describe the bald man's cuisine, Paul rued the day, almost twenty years before, that the editor of the Christian music magazine---where Paul interned in college---praised him for being a good writer. A few years later

JEFFREY ELLINGER

Paul received an encouraging email
from someone else which he often cited
as his main reason for starting to write.
Keep it up, the note read, the Lord has
blessed you with talent. That
compliment was one of the last things
he heard from her, a girl he met on
MySpace at the beginning of his time in
Nebraska on the ranch. A week before
receiving that message he visited her in
Alabama, and the day he returned to
work she broke up with him over text
because, as she wrote, You just don't
have the right heart for spiritual
leadership.

On the couch in the apartment near the
cold lake, Paul went to his sleepy social
media account and saw his updates
from the day before, about a blogging
platform that made a habit out of
excoriating the people they didn't like—
even if those people stood for the same
principles the progressive blogging
platform purported to stand for—and
capriciously praising those who stood
for the opposite of those principles. The
nationally known website had posted a
controversial article that went against
every fiber of the liberal principles they
said they represented. After criticizing
them the day before, Paul sat on the
couch, waiting for his phone to ping with
positive reinforcement. I should delete

these, he thought, disconcerted by his attempt to enter a conversation dominated by those who had established an audience in the conversation. What if I lived without social media? Paul entertained this thought as if he suddenly had become someone who could live without status. To live without an audience, yes, he dreamed, to be a man. Paul's father never used social media. He raised a family and cattle and maintained the best lawn in town. He did good work, and if people noticed, they noticed. If they didn't, that was on them.

What if I followed that sort of brand, Paul wondered. People might call me chef and my parents would be interviewed by a public television host and tell a man in a sweater vest and bow tie that their son always had such a passion: *We just knew that whatever he set his mind to, he'd do.* I would not be sitting on the couch hoping that just one person will affirm what I have said. Paul sat on the couch and balded. Navigating on his phone, he came across a water-skiing squirrel. The absurdity made Paul want to delete everything, but he managed only to get up and eat and after that go to the bedroom, where he watched a video of four women and two men who went to the gym supposedly to get in shape. Their ruddy smiles full of hope, they had tan skin, except for the whiteness of their fit backsides.

—

After another day of data entry Paul searched for when the next Steam sale would be and found it'd be at the end of the month, the same as always. Then he pored over a story about a playboy who inherited money from his father and used that money to film well-endowed women shooting automatic rifles in the desert and quivering from the recoil of each bullet through the chamber. Ben Drazil should be arrested, Paul thought. For what crimes, he did not know, just that the man should be put in jail. Mai Topez, a self-help guru who bragged about the books he read and the Lamborghinis he drove in ads before the videos Paul watched of yoga women stretching and massaging each other, should be put in jail as well, perhaps even made to share a cell with Drazil, so they would be forced to brag to each other for the rest of their lives and become increasingly angry that a man could exist who thought he had it better.

Another hour went by and Paul still lay on the couch, overcome with the paradox of Schrödinger. He knew that if his life depended on explaining without stammering what the experiment and subsequent theory meant, he would not be able to do it. It would be a lot of him saying, Well, you see, and, You know what I mean, interspersed with truncated ideas loosely related to the topic. Paul needed more than being on the couch and not knowing anything. A meme on Drazil's social media account had said, Stop Doing the Thing You Don't Want to Do. Long ago that kind of schlock made sense to Paul, back when he earnestly tried to live his best life by working full-time while searching for love, then, as he got older, by working full-time and writing every day. At some point he realized the way to get the things you want is by being born having the things you want.

It is too late for that, Paul thought. The couch smelled only of him. No traces of his lady were left. If she had stayed she would have been curled up beside him, on her tablet, surfing for deals at organic clothing companies based in Silver Lake, Los Angeles. The apartment was dark except for the lamplight, and with the occasional hum of a car speeding on Prospect Avenue, Paul deemed the room pleasant. "Pleasant" was the only word he could think of to describe it, which brought him back to someone he saw in Minneapolis. She was born in Canada to Iranian parents, and by the time they met she had grown to possess an intimidating form. She taught cinema at the University of Minnesota and gave hope to Paul at the beginning of online dating. He listened when she said pleasant was a pointless word, and he agreed with her, but for years afterward he used it as much as possible to spite her, as if from a romantic grave.

We were never that close, Paul thought, and I am bald and do not know influential fiction writers like Lily Braun or Samantha Mandler. I am not gender fluid. I have a beard, and I am bald and divorced. I am white and have so few followers, and even the ones I do have do not care. I do not know any Jews.

Paul thought unshareable content while Tyler sexted and Mike programmed. Mike smelled vaguely of lotion and Tyler smelled of motor oil. Mike shaved his chest, leaving prickly hairs jutting out. On Tyler's chest, only a tuft, with the smallest patch on his lower back. Tyler was tan and fit. Mike, pale and overweight. They both thought of themselves as great men. Paul, almost totally bald, sat on the couch without his

lady rooting her feet under his thighs
and between the cushions of the couch
to keep her toes warm. She is on the
beaches of Formentera, Paul thought.
Or she is hiking in the Badlands with the
Sioux. She's here or she's there, and it
went on and on like that.

—

The week ended. The sun shone on a
Saturday. Skies drawn in blue like with a
crayon. Inside the apartment Paul lay on
the couch watching a comedy from the
late 1980s. In the movie a boy casually
used the term "homo" to rib a younger
sister who drew pictures of Thor and
adorned her wall with posters of the
Norse god's face. The older brother
came in grinning and called Thor a
homo, and that was fine, not so long
ago. Paul wondered, without moving,
what might be considered gauche the
same number of years in the future.
Cringing, he thought of how authors
from the past used the N-word, and Paul
wondered, What's the point of anything?
There seemed to be a good chance that
whatever he wrote would one day be
uncouth and readers would shake their
heads in disapproval or hoot with glee
over a term that had seemed anodyne in
the past but had since become divisive.

JEFFREY ELLINGER

I have so many excuses, Paul thought, as he continued to watch *Adventures in Babysitting*. He wanted Elisabeth Shue to be in love with him, like with Ralph Macchio in *The Karate Kid*. In her youthful state, with her wavy hair and soothing voice, she seemed perfect. He imagined her as a good wife and mother.

The day was almost warm, making the not-doing-anything all the more grating. Walk to the used bookstore again? Go to the coffee shop by the lake and gawk at the backsides of college girls and full-figured moms? Peer at the waters of Lake Michigan? These things Paul had done, and the more he did them the more it seemed he did them as a way of distracting himself from the fact that he was doing nothing, and that made him worry that he did them because he had nothing to do. That was Saturday.

On Sunday Paul called his mother and kept the conversation short. He worried that if he lingered he might let slip that his lady had left. Sundays with her had not been much better. As a couple they wanted more than to walk to the bookstore or to the lake or coffee shop. Sometimes the indecision got so bad they would sit imprisoned on the couch for much of the morning and into the afternoon, both hoping the other would come up with a plan. Tyler and Mike had finished balding. Their Sundays could be free of yearning. They had become what they would become, and if someone saw them they would see that these men looked satisfied. Since he no longer went to church with his devout live-in girlfriend, Mike spent the morning programming. Feet on the coffee table, every so often he would bring out plates of food and slop over them and watch television for a few minutes before muting it, putting his feet back on the coffee table, and getting back to the lines of code. Later, Mike stopped for a few minutes to pretend to listen to his large-breasted girlfriend talk about what happened at church. As a man with a wife and child in the house, Tyler hunkered down in his garage. He tinkered with his Jeep, his phone nearby so he could be there to see when it lit up and to respond—after wiping his oily hands with a rag—to another from his past with *thats nice id fuck u hard*. His Sunday full of manly pleasures, with his wife not wanting more. He had given her everything she could want. Mysteries come along with so much plenty.

JEFFREY ELLINGER

Paul's lady who had left had never experienced a perfect Sunday. They came close early on, when they drove out to Holy Hill to see the leaves, or when they went on a tour of the New Glarus brewery, or when during their last spring together they shuffled around the Capitol building with the mindless hippies in Madison. But even on those weekends it was like they had to fill the day with activities in order to distract themselves from the more overbearing truism: *I am balding and so we will always be in a state of unrest.* Paul put that line in the notes on his phone. Maybe one day he'd return to flesh out his musings, put them to good use. For now there were well-endowed yoga teachers massaging each other. They said they lived in Texas. He imagined them closer.

—

Finished with data entry and back on the couch—the weather gray, nothing to do other than cleaning that he no longer really needed to do—Paul lost himself in an enjoyable state where everything seemed possible, where the idea of quitting his job and writing full-time—for whom or what about, he hardly knew— seemed capable of becoming a reality.

The selling of his car and purchasing of a better bicycle, the moving out of the apartment where he and his lady once lived, starting fresh, this time with roommates. A lifestyle piece in the *Times* said that in the future we'll all have roommates, and Paul liked the idea of being ahead of the curve. At first, he guessed, there'd be a certain shame—of being older, divorced—but once his younger comrades understood the aims of their well-traveled boarder, Paul imagined, he could settle into a routine that allowed for expression and created latitude for living, as opposed to driving in traffic to be on time for a job he hated. That kind of encumbered cycle could be put in the past, back in the fifties, when everything seemed idyllic but was rotted at its core.

The American Dream is a farce, Paul entered into his phone, a commercial packaged and sold to us. The observation, like something from a bad screenplay, was one he would never go back and read again. He started to type another vapid thought about capitalism, but he became distracted and instead started to watch a video of men brawling on the grounds of the Kentucky Derby. Everyone stood in a circle. They wore pink shorts and pastel-blue polo shirts or vice versa, and in the ensuing melee a blond-haired college boy was kicked in the head. Paul searched the comments but could not find an update on the young man's condition.

As if he'd received a thumping of his own, Paul's fantasy of being an Important Creative crystallized as a distinct impossibility. He did not have connections for a freelance gig or an advanced degree. He was not a member of the gilded class, and did not post on communist blogs. Worst of all, if someone could have measured his heart, they would have seen that Paul did not believe his novel on the plight of the balding man in America would become a sensation. Quitting his job, Paul knew, would end up amounting to him masturbating during the day instead of at night, and within a few months he would be poor. Paul on the couch acutely understood this: that the words he wrote from that second until the moment he died would not be varied enough or come in an order that would lead him to the kind of recognition he vigorously wanted. Having a child could revive his outlook, but his lady was gone, and with her any chance of becoming a stay-at-home novelist while she worked on her soap-making business and later taught her yoga classes in a barn, near a farmhouse

outside of Madison that had been
handed down to them by her
grandfather.

Being a dad could start a new chapter in
my life, Paul thought, desperate for his
lady to come back and at the same time
wanting to rend his tight clothes from his
body. A new ball of life could grow up
and hurdle over all the mistakes I made.
Paul entertained that possibility for a
second but in the next he saw it as the
most tired idea, and he rutted in the
cushions. It was in these moments after
the cubicle that Paul was hardest on
himself. His gut hung over the
waistband of his new work pants. After
being at the data entry job so long, he
needed assemble a wardrobe. When he
first started Paul told his lady he would
only need the three dress shirts he
already owned. Business-casual, they
call it, he told her in jest.

Why is it impossible to lose weight?
Paul thought, genuine in his frustration
as he lay there on the couch. He lived in
penury with his lady gone, and now
penury seemed wrong, as if he had
learned the word that morning and was
eager to use it, like a junior high boy at a
private school trying to impress the
senior editors of the newspaper, as if he

belonged in a Loah Timbeck film, as if he were Liesel Merwig's doppelganger. I am Liesel's jangly homemade earrings, Paul thought, emulating the masculine author of the book about underground thumb-war clubs that Paul read as a teenager. At least Paul knew this much: being well-read amounted to discarding your favorites until you reached the age of about thirty-five, at which point tastes were ossified or calcified or whatever the word was and you had given up on reading anyway.

For a few minutes Paul toyed with the idea of sending out mean tweets about overly praised Important Creatives but soon gave it up, knowing he would never have the gall. He stopped typing in his phone and closed his eyes. His belly was full after devouring cereal and leftover rotisserie chicken and sodas. He had reverted to the atrocious eating habits of bachelordom, when staples were brats and Cokes and ramen noodles and hamburgers. His lady had brought colors in: green salads, the red pants she suggested he buy, the black dress shoes to go with, as she told him, so many things. In that time early on with her Paul felt like he would change, like he could live up to the potential his parents once saw. Now Paul drifted out of wakefulness and into half-dreaming.

In this state he could be Tyler or Mike,
with the kind of bald head flexible
masseuses rubbed with their oiled
fingers on camera in a well-lit room with
impeccable fêng shui as a rescue dog
ambled in, looking for treats. Paul did
what he always did and fell asleep after.
Then the next day came, and another
after that.

—

There are so many lucky others in the
world, thought Paul, on the couch after
work as the property manager
vacuumed outside his door. The grating
sound seemed interminable. Still, Paul
was glad. The white noise drowned out
the whistling of the property manager.
Paul also took some solace in the fact
that he lived in a place where they
vacuumed too much, rather than too
little. He could not think about how much
longer he would be able to afford the
apartment. Instead he put his earbuds
back in and watched as a smooth prick,
not fully erect, slid into an athletic
woman's backside. She pushed in
rhythm against the man, as if keeping
time to a metronome, and moaned with
each thrust, her nubs of breasts twirling
in erratic patterns, her sliver of a thong
to one side. At the end of the amateur

production she asked her boyfriend to come inside her, and he obliged. Then he took the camera from its tripod and zoomed in on his love oozing out of her. He must be proud, Paul thought, to see how much enjoyment he could give.

Seconds later, after finishing on himself, Paul fell into a daydream and woke to the fluid slithering down his side. He got up, showered, and went to the kitchen for brats, chips, and pop. Done with eating and with nothing else to do, he went back to bed. With his lady gone, Paul did not have to stay awake until she came home so they could have a talk where she explained the ways in which she was not happy and he told her the ways in which he was doing his best but could never seem to catch a break. Those talks always ended with a long pause and him asking, What are you thinking right now? Next they'd have a silence where neither knew what to say, and it would become a standoff to determine who would be so callous as to get up first and embark on another task in the apartment to determine who would be crowned the person most affected by the tension. Those emotional battles Paul did not miss. Free to be a loser, Paul saw going back to sleep as a loss to no one. In the bathroom at work earlier in the day, the notion had struck him that if he were a real man he would not write a self-referential roman à clef, some solipsistic self-published autobiographical bildungsroman about what it was like to be himself, but a novel about what it was like to be anyone else. He would go back into his history, reach down in his genealogy and discover what it was like for his ancestors to emigrate to America and settle along a river and build a church made of stone and till the land to be fruitful. He would have paragraphs full of words learned in a language class, and not just *lefse* and *lutefisk* and *uffda*, but *dod* and *snakker* and *trodde*, and he would italicize them and make it known that the characters in this expansive work about Norwegian life in South Dakota in the late 1880s spoke the language, and he, the narrator, was merely a cipher for their noedofor.

But *noedofor* was not a word, in Norwegian or any other language. It was the best Paul could do, conjure nonsense from the empyrean void, and in that bathroom at work, where cockroaches scurried across the floor if the lights got turned off for a few minutes, he knew that if he wanted to be considered great—if he wanted to live in a brownstone in Brooklyn next door to wealthy commentators on societal ills—

he would have to be the author of that Scandinavian-slash-Dakotan novel, and only then would Knausgaard Himself be the other neighbor and come over and ask for *fluederfluff*, and only then would they talk late into the night about literary greats like Flaubert and Oe and Yates, until it was time to accept one of the invitations from the graduate students in Greenpoint who practiced yoga and yearned to be taken in the ass by a real novelist.

That perverse clarity stayed with Paul, and at home in the apartment he dropped himself on the couch, where he scrolled through his phone as he listened to the vacuuming. A number of people in contorted positions piqued his interest and took him down a path where the only thing he saw ahead of him was pleasure. Moments later he was sleeping, but before drifting off he thought, She was always saying sorry but never for anything that mattered. The line seemed poetic in half-sleep, though when Paul woke he had forgotten it and a familiar dread returned. All he could think of was his own death.

—

I actually like dandelions, Paul said to
no one as he walked from his car to the
apartment after parking near a field of
yellow. The sun shone. Young men who
looked like they belonged in a folk band
mowed the lawn of a palatial mansion
overlooking the cold lake. They wore
plaid flannels and brimmed hats and
had beards. Paul walked past them in
the late afternoon. Puffy clouds hovered
above the skyline. He breathed in the
fresh-cut grass and saw out past where
they mowed, to a field of dandelions,
and he did say out loud, I actually like
dandelions.

Paul's father did not allow a single
weed. At first sight they were dug out of
the lawn, and as a youth Paul spent
hours on weekends in the summer
pulling crabgrass. Now, as a man, it
struck Paul that dandelions were pretty.
A fey thought, he knew, but true all the
same, how the yellow flowers burst with
color against the new green. They could
be playthings for lovers on a blanket, or
for teens tricking their friends into
opening their mouths and sticking them
inside, or for children to pick and blow
away and create more of what is called
a weed but did not seem like one to
Paul at that moment. The warm weather
put him under a spell, like a cat nestling
on that spot on the couch where light

streams in on a winter day. Love existed in the world, and he thought about how great things could be.

These Elysian rumblings had started earlier, when Paul arrived at the office. He skipped his normal routine of sitting in his car in the parking lot for a good ten minutes, listening to blubbering sports radio while building up the guts needed to enter the monochromatic building with its farms of cubicles. Instead, he jumped out and walked in, following a fair auburn-haired creature in a blue-and-pink silk blouse, a black skirt, sheer black nylons, and black high heels. Over the past weeks Paul had noticed she took the same elevator at about the same time most mornings. On many days he missed her, but on the days he caught her they talked, once about the weather, and another time about how weird the floor he got off on looked, like the set of a horror movie, she had said, and Paul had laughed too hard. Today he ran inside, and for the first time he noticed a tattoo on her meaty calf: flowers twisted into a decorative shape. Jogging down the hallway, Paul got to the elevator before the door closed.

She trusts me, Paul thought. She would never go up alone like this if she didn't. She would have never pressed the button to keep it open. They stood in the steel box no one else in the building used. Paul loved that she would choose the road less taken.

Two? she asked.

Paul also loved her large nose, like the nose of a girl he once dated for a month in Minneapolis, who had the most beautiful nipples he had ever seen.

Three, he said. Thanks. Secretly, Paul was crushed that she did not remember his floor. He had hoped she'd remember, that all the details of their interactions were imprinted on her. The devastation lasted only for a second, as Paul peeked at her scrolling through her phone. He fantasized that she was ignoring him as a coy trick, belying her desire to bite her lip and throw down her device and lunge at his belt buckle, like a caged animal let loose, and put his prick in her mouth, and once the elevator opened and the door closed behind them they would find a room where he'd pull down her skirt and take her with her high heels still on, and after, on a patch of clean carpet, spend time admiring her red bra, visible beneath her half-unbuttoned blouse.

The elevator door opened. Paul got off at his floor. The woman did not look. She went up to a better-paying job. Paul did not know when he would see her again, and that was disheartening, but his spirits lifted while he entered data, thinking of so many other beautiful redheads and sensitive big-butted readers of *The Easter Parade* and hairy-pitted artists in the world. As Paul walked home along the lake, he sensed himself being pulled off the ground. He saw all of the dandelions in the city, the countryside in Wisconsin, and the greater world. Glorious, he dreamed, and he even managed to write notes in his phone before passing out on the couch that evening, notes that could be the beginning of something that went: redhead in elevator, sheer tights covering up rose tattoo on meaty calf, pointy nose, looks like the law student I once dated who was always friendly, looking at her phone to cover up the animal desire to leap at my belt, talked about the weather once and that seemed to be a prelude to afternoons unbuttoning her blouses and pushing down her high-waisted skirts, and afterward admiring her bra askew, her

pale belly with my love in messy
puddles.

———

I could either create or masturbate, Paul
typed into his phone in the solitary
apartment. His left ear hurt after another
day of loud music. Afraid to keep both
earbuds in—in case one of the big
mamas said something he didn't hear
and they came back and saw on his
phone's screen a half-naked woman in
the act of languid stretching—he played
the music loud in one ear. Imperative,
Paul believed, to combat the
inexhaustible conversations about what
everyone would be getting for lunch.
The beats had been at tympanum-
bursting levels that day, and now his ear
hurt as he yawned on the couch,
contemplating a search for Ivone Sexy
Amateur or Layla Rivera Tight Booty. A
story that day from the endless content
factory highlighted a Democratic
candidate in Virginia who screenshot his
official blog, and those were the titles of
two of the tabs in his browser. A part of
Paul did not want to search, as he knew
that afterward there would be a hole in
his soul. The rhyming frustrated him,
and he switched to thinking something
he had thought a million times before: I

wonder if all of my touching myself
made me lose my hair.

In Charleston, Tyler did it to supple
forms sent from Chicago via satellites in
space while his wife took care of their
baby. Tyler had convinced himself he
did no wrong, when his bride had
agreed to nothing. Tyler heard what he
wanted to hear and did what he wanted
to do. All the while Mike touched his
own body but would never admit to it,
unlike Tyler, who would proudly
announce it in a way that encouraged
someone else to do it for him. Mike
connived conquests, like his current
Christian girlfriend, who a year before
had woken one Saturday morning next
to a snoring, deodorant-smelling body—
Mike exuded a tangy odor—with
eyeliner meant to gain her attention
smeared on the pillow. There was
shaved chest hair in her face and a bald
head like another penis, with bad breath
blowing on her like a fan reminding her
with every puff how she had misjudged
the night before. The only consolation
was that this Mike guy was not the kind
of guy who would spring for brunch. He
had to get to coding, he'd said the night
before, or was it up north for hunting?
She foggily recalled—while mounting
the courage to slink out of bed—that
Mike had said the following at the bar:

Space movies are gay and so are video games. And, kind of sarcastically: Men are better than women at everything except for tits. Catching her ample construction in his full-body mirror, all color left her face.

Paul on the couch stopped dreaming of pretend bald men and thought of authors: Yates, Salter, Percy, Céline, Berriault, Pym, Cather, Brennan, Bernhard, Maxwell, and the others who made art out of their struggles. Unlike Salter and Yates, Paul had never done anything so masculine as enter the service, and he never took the Hippocratic Oath, like Percy or Céline. On top of that, Paul had never sold a thing in his life, other than in grade school when he signed up members of his extended family to buy candy bars to fund band trips to Disney World. Once for a brief period in Minneapolis he worked at a steelyard with ex-convicts, and he perdured years of delivering packages, and long before that he'd been sensitive enough to try to save the soul of anyone who didn't believe in Christ. He moved around many times and one day found a job in Portland, where he met his wife, who left him. Later so did all his hair, and then his lady in the rusted city along the cold lake, too. Now on the couch he was overwhelmed by curiosity, to know what kind of backside Layla boasted, to see how innocent yet ravenous Ivone could be. On the kitchen table there were bills to be paid. In the refrigerator, no food other than a very close to empty bottle of ketchup. Paul could not think of how to describe the bottle other than very close to empty. The ineptitude made him want to forget his life, but then desire lit up his brain and the parts that wanted to try stayed dull, dark.

—

A year went by or maybe more and Paul sat in a coffee shop after work to see if he could be jarred into usefulness. In his past of delivering packages Paul would often brush up against upscale citizens at coffee shops, typing on laptops and frivolously updating their social media accounts, searching for former or future lovers. In all those coffee shops Paul longed to be important enough to have a silver computer that looked like the other silver computers. To have enough confidence to lug it into a public space and enough money to buy a coffee he wouldn't drink and then to type unimportant words that seemed important to everyone else, now and then peering at those who had chosen to do the same thing. A congregation, a type of church, Paul typed into his phone, sitting on a hard chair in the back room of the coffee shop. The drivel continued. A gathering of devoted participants, he wrote, giving of their time and worshipping in their own way. Their higher power is to have status among their peers. Paul stopped typing. Then came the upbraiding: Jesus, he thought, can I really be writing about writing in a coffee shop?

Loud conversation from a group around a long table interrupted the self-reproach. They talked of putting on their leader hats and being one and done. Listening over the ambient music in his earbuds, Paul envied their privileged talks about nothing. Only those with okay-paying jobs could have an inconsequential meeting like theirs. Never could Paul manage to find decent jobs when searching online. All he could apply for was work that paid a few dollars more than minimum wage, like delivery driving and manual labor, the kind of work where the well-educated managers feet away from him now talked in offices upstairs about how to make the laborers downstairs more efficient. Those managers held meetings in coffee shops. They vacationed in Hawaii. They worried about how their 401(k)s performed.

Goddamn fruit flies, Paul thought, and shooed one away. He should have stayed at the other table. He wondered: Why am I always so uncertain about where I am?

Paul could see that the managers had biked to the coffee shop; their helmets hung on the arms of their chairs. They drank coffee but had their own Nalgenes filled with water. If the people from Paul's work near the fairgrounds were to hold a meeting like the one in front of him, the table would be littered with Diet Coke cans and candy bars and homemade sweets nibbled on out of obligation. Paul had recently received a promotion at the social services company, and he now wrote grant proposals. The new work equaled the data entry in monotony and made him wish he'd never lobbied so hard for the marginal raise that barely kept him in the apartment he once lived in with his lady. She'd encouraged him to go for the job before she left, and now that he had it he wished he could go back, but he was stuck, and nothing could be done.

Nothing can be done, Paul thought, and
I want her. His staring was all they
would ever have. Paul would not get up
and speak to her, even though their
eyes had met twice as she cuddled with
her boyfriend. She and her man stood in
the coffee shop by the railing above a
huge pump that once flushed pollutants
out of the water for the city of
Milwaukee. Jesus, Paul thought, she is
blessed. The one he yearned for wore a
blue-and-white striped shirt and a pair of
jeans that would cause a scandal within
the context of a conservative workplace,
maybe even cause enough internal
discussions to prompt an email from
human resources. She had a plain face,
Paul noticed, and that might have been
what made her attainable to the stocky
man who put his hand around her waist
and down into her back pocket. Paul
lusted after her and at the same time
knew he would never see here again,
the woman with the backside that could
make a man weep with devotion, and
that made the wanting all the worse.

I steal the parts about backsides, Paul
thought, and all the rest is regurgitating
my own thoughts and calling it fiction,
and I complain I am not recognized?

JEFFREY ELLINGER

I deserve nothing, Paul continued. A tall professional man sat at a small table in a nook in the corner, away from the table of coworkers. Paul had chosen this room thinking no one would be coming back here; the only other seating available, drenched in sunlight, would blind a computer screen. The tall professional sat in the light and chewed on a muffin and sipped from his coffee as he squinted at a book on the Tao of, well, Paul couldn't read the rest. He googled "The Tao of" and a book on Eastern religions popped up. Paul thought again of the round-bottomed one with the chubby boyfriend. Whatever Tyler or Mike did at that moment was fine. Let them be, he thought. Too many problems polluted his brain to bother with imaginary people not burdened by their baldness.

That stout man with the curvy white girlfriend has hair, Paul wrote in his phone. I bet he buys her sweet iced coffees and Thai takeout and pays for whatever she does to keep her rump meaty, and they barely ever argue. I bet he makes twice as much money as she does, and that is why they are touching each other in public. The woman, Paul typed, should have a job that is not so taxing that she doesn't have time to care for her appearance. She should have a job like part-time Acroyoga teacher, a job that grants freedom, as money will never be her worry. She has to be free to pursue her passion of being fit. Being in charge, making money, hair, that's what matters.

Looking back at what he'd written, Paul grimaced. He got up and left the coffee shop in a fugue of longing. That evening he watched *American Splendor* and was emboldened at first to see the similarities: baldness—Pekar dealt with his by growing his hair out on the sides and allowing the tufts to run wild; a quotidian life in Rust Belt cities the rest of the country pitied, toiling away at a mundane job while trying to make art out of misery. Years ago, Paul did not empathize with Pekar's lot. At the time Paul first saw the film, that kind of dreary life seemed comical in the same way it was comical to yuppie puppets like Dave Letterman who used Pekar as a running joke. Back in college, and for a good few years after, Paul had too much in front of him to believe he could ever end up bald and alone with hair on his back, working at a job he hated. Fifteen years after the movie came out, though, Paul saw more of himself in the cartoonist: a love of great literature, the phonies he saw everywhere, the drive to create something true. But Paul was not

half as popular as Pekar, and that was
the redeeming quality in the
cantankerous artist. As the movie
continued Paul realized he shared only
the bleak aspects: divorce, loneliness,
balding, oppressive day job. Worst of all,
Robert Crumb, the editor and champion
of Pekar, would not be walking through
the door anytime soon.

Perhaps, Paul thought, the one thing
holding me back is my lack of multiple
wives. Great artists get married twice,
Paul thought, sometimes three times or
more. They get older and their partners
become younger and that shows an
ascension of status which enables the
old artist to attract another young bride
with a jaunty step, ruddy cheeks, and a
full backside. But Paul had only the sad
day job. He did not have, unlike Pekar, a
catalog of artistic work to show a
graduate student. Pekar and Bellow and
other libertines bedded neophytes that
way. Sophisticated nymphets could not
help but be awed when meeting the one
behind the creation, and the sagging
artist used that weakness in the young
one's personality—a weakness that
usually served as a shield against the
advances of normal men—to thrust a
limp sword through her and bring her
back to his atelier with rows of books
she has never read, and soon enough

she is undressed and splayed on the leather couch.

Paul, lacking an atelier or a leather couch, lived in the same apartment he once lived in with his lady, who was very gone. Nothing of her remained other than a ribbon hanging on the door, a bottle of wine from her parents—and something else, Paul thought the next afternoon, in the coffee shop with the pump down below, but there was nothing else. At the end of each of their three years together she'd wanted to move out, to find a different place that would give them a breath of fresh air. In the coffee shop Paul remembered talking about the application they'd filled out to live in a refurbished brick condo in Walker's Point. That night he played his baseball video game, sitting in a chair pulled close to the television, while she scrolled through her tablet.

Why didn't we fill out your information? she asked. Paul thought he had made a good argument to allay her fears, but she was rightfully concerned. Why didn't we fill out your information too? she asked again. We might have screwed ourselves by not doing that, Paul.

JEFFREY ELLINGER

Paul, not as bald then, tried to pay
attention to his game, but his lady's
worrying put him half in the imaginary
world and half in the real one, in a state
where he could do nothing in either.
Wanting to escape, he tried to lose
himself in the fake baseball game
instead of the real, disappointed woman
behind him.

Why didn't we do that? she asked from
the couch. I'm the main breadwinner,
but that doesn't mean you shouldn't add
to our total. That only would have
helped. You shouldn't be embarrassed
by what you make, Paul.

Paul's vision narrowed into a tunnel, and
the digital pitcher pitched a meatball to
Joe Mauer. Paul, as Mauer, whiffed, like
in a dream where he could never swing
fast enough. Paul sneezed. Bless me,
Paul said quietly, and his lady said,
Yeah, but honey, okay, don't be
embarrassed. Why did we not have you
fill out your information too?

It is what it is at this point, Paul said out
of obligation, fearing soon his lady
would get mad at him for not engaging,
though she had said she liked having
him play his games to get his mind off
things. He made what he made.

In the coffee shop years later Paul
packed up his computer, and when he
got back to the apartment Pekar's ghost
floated through the small rooms. After a
big swig from a cheap bottle of wine—
not the one from her parents, which he
would never open—Paul collapsed on
the couch and took out his phone.
Women playing yoga teachers covered
themselves in oil and satisfied men with
heads full of hair. Minutes later, as a
pair of triangular breasts moved in figure
eights, Paul did not want.

In the coffee shop after another day of
work near the fairgrounds Paul wanted
to write an epic poem with the word
"elegy" in the title, but all he did was
drink iced tea and play his fantasy role-
playing game. Earlier, while he was in
line, the barista had said to a coworker:
Of course I look different, man, I'm not
in high school anymore, then
acknowledged Paul by dance-walking to
the register and asking, What do you
need, man? Paul quietly spoke his
order, after which the teen barista ran
his hand through his blond hair and
flipped the plastic cup and said, How
about a large? Paul said okay as plainly
as he could, and the worker filled the
plastic cup with tea and ice and set it

down. Here you go, bro, he said, then vanished into the kitchen like a specter. Paul walked away impressed by the young man, thinking perhaps he had been paying unironic homage to Tom Cruise in *Cocktail*.

After sipping tea and playing his game and not writing a poem, Paul walked out of the coffee shop. He had a split-second opportunity to leave the door open for a creature he believed to be stunning, but he let it close, and she had to open the door herself. He walked to the lake in guilt. Once his lady said: I wish you'd be more of a gentleman. Another time she told Paul he lacked a frontal lobe. Walking along the lake, Paul knew she must have been right, about his brain's chemistry and everything else. He found an open bench and glanced at the endless water, the ominous largeness of it, before turning his attention to his phone, where he read about the website that represented power in the world of becoming an Important Creative. Paul wanted all the Important Creatives to fail. He knew he would take a sick pleasure in their downfall. Those who got paid to have opinions and thoughts had made it.

Pathetic, Paul typed in his phone. All those bloggers who'd been bullied in high school had gone to college and majored in journalism and gotten an internship in New York, then they got lucky and met the right person, so that one day they got an email from a friend that said, Hey man, website's hiring and I totally know the editor, you should apply. So they did, and got the job, and were given a pulpit to use their words instead of physical strength, and if they could they would out every last person who had wronged them in high school, calling them awful names like fag or whore—even if the blogger wrote for the vertical that empowered women or championed equal rights—or, in lieu of that, they bullied anyone they could, and the more churn their stories got the more money their posts made and the more followers they acquired and the more media contacts they accrued, so that one day they could secure a book deal like others who had blogged about where celebrities get their coffee, and that would lead them to a boring novel and then a collection of bland short stories.

Pathetic, Paul thought; I want to be them. He clicked the lock button and his phone went black. He thought for a second about walking over to where jagged rocks met the jutting shore. What would it be like, he wondered, to let my injured body drift to the deep, where it would be broken down and become food for fish? Paul picked up his bag. Night was coming. He did not want to be out alone. He'd been born slight, like a writer, and his lady had often given him grief for it, saying she could beat him up. He hated his arms, but no matter how many CrossFit workouts he completed Paul stayed the same discouraging size. What can be done about how I am, Paul thought, going up the hill to the apartment. I wish I were skinny but I am not. I am beefy and broad. And that was true, unlike what he'd thought moments before. Paul looked down at his significant belly. No one noticed as he walked into the building.

—

Back at the coffee shop with the outdated industrial pump, Paul wrapped himself in the past. Laptop open—but only to play his fantasy video game—he passively thought about fights. One partner says they have to get out, he thought, while clicking his mouse to equip and upgrade a sword with a powerful rune. They say You don't love me anymore, when they know the other person loves them dearly, because they want to make themselves feel better about leaving. Paul kept playing his game. The fights stayed in the past. They fought about everything and nothing. About their fights they fought, and about Paul looking at others. They fought about her not feeling defended at social engagements. They fought in Chicago and Hawaii and New Orleans and across the Upper Middle West, on interstates and side roads, in bed and standing up. They fought always for reasons he did not understand, and that caused them to fight more. They fought and fought and the processing after their fights always helped her feel better and him worse. They never fought about his lack of hair, but he feared that was what their fights were all about.

Whatever is done is done, Paul repeated in his head while playing his game. Whatever will happen is what will happen.

His hair, Paul believed, had fallen out because of transgressions, for being rude and weak. Those transgressions contained the salt that eroded his scalp. The day was cloudy and warm near the cold lake and Paul had never been a fighter pilot like Salter, or an infantryman

like Salinger, who carried his typewriter
to the front. He had not been a B.A.R.
Man like Yates. An hour later and alone,
Paul packed up and walked out of the
coffee shop. He paced along the lake.
Bred allegiance to worshipping in
subdued tones allowed solitude that
morning. In a few hours families in
pedal-driven carts pushing baby strollers
would clog the path. Homeless men
would sell water, making Paul feel guilty
for never buying a bottle. Paul could
almost see Mike and Tyler across the
water, living their accomplished lives. I
could root my head into the ground,
Paul thought. Be in the dirt like an
animal. I have hurt others, he thought.
That's why I must hurt. That's why I
have to be uneasy.

The sun peeked out from behind the
clouds, but that alone could not color a
novel. The sun peeked out and the
breeze was gentle and for a second
Paul did not think about how bald he
had become. He did not want to retrace
steps. Then the clouds snapped back
together, like someone had completed a
puzzle, and Paul thought of his lady,
who was gone, on a beach in Croatia,
perhaps. It was all he could think about,
his lady who was gone. Paul's mind was
small and he thought of passive verbs.
Whatever is done is done. Whatever will

happen is what will happen. Paul got up and walked to the edge. How unearned an ending. He stepped back, and talked to himself the whole walk home.

—

If he ever wanted to be considered an Important Creative, Paul was sure, he had to care that a boxer had passed. But Paul could not find the will to click on any of the articles splashed online, nor did he sense a mite of sadness at the boxer's passing or submit a positive comment in response to one of the paeans about how the boxer had been the greatest person who ever lived. Paul did not believe in spirits, not anymore, and he did not understand the fascination with slobbery eulogies for those who in life were philandering bullies. Never are the lengthy obituaries for a regular joe or jane who lived their life working humbly, he wrote in his phone in the coffee shop, treating his or her fellow man or woman with respect while doing their level best to leave the earth in a better condition. Paul hated the overwrought tributes but at the same time he wanted, when he was gone, to have one. Just one, Paul wrote, not an internet full of them, not like the racist boxers and opiate addicts. Only one,

about how I inspired a limp-wristed
weakling to be a writer of
autobiographical fiction.

Paul lowered his phone to observe the
group of college students to his right.
Loud and brash, they must have had, as
his lady once jokingly described girls
that age, fresh pussies. Paul sat there
not understanding why it was good to be
proud to be anything. Everything was
determined at birth. The college girls
had not done a thing to make
themselves anything other than what
they were. Paul would never be an
Important Creative. He played with his
phone and could not drum up the ire to
defend the plight of men in the city who
shot other men in the city. He did not
think it was the fault of those men. He
thought it was the fault of evolution,
bringing us to this point in history where
we think we have free will to yearn for
more than what is assigned to us. Paul's
right foot hurt, and that bothered him so
much he wanted to take off his boot and
throw it down into the artisanal hole
where the coffee shop kept the
equipment that once pumped the city's
water into, or maybe out of, Lake
Michigan. Paul did not know. He didn't
know a thing. He was a self-involved
bald white bearded man obsessed with
the word "solipsistic." Paul wore boots

he could not afford but had bought in a
fit of self-pity, and now he wanted to
throw them down the hole. A young
woman with round glasses and a silky
ponytail—wearing white Converse and
black spandex pants and a gray t-shirt—
walked by, and Paul wanted her to
come over and fix the extra material
someone at the factory in Red Wing had
mistakenly added and after that take his
prick out of his jeans and work on him
until he could think nothing. The college
girls getting up turned his attention.
They left their computers and bags and
phones at the table, believing no one
could ever do them harm. They wore
shorts so short their white pockets
extended past the denim edges. Paul
lusted after their smooth legs, without
any cellulite, so smooth it seemed as
though they wore nylons, and for a
second he forgot about his baldness
and his lady who left and the ill-fitting
boots and thought instead about the
halter tops of those college girls and
their straight brown hair and how their
asses must taste like nothing at all. He
ground the right side of his boot into the
wooden floor and cursed God for
bequeathing to one of His children a
heart that did not care about the death
of boxers who beat women. The young
woman with the silky ponytail and white
Converse walked by once more, and

JEFFREY ELLINGER

Paul could have sworn this time he heard her giggling, like she could read the mind of the bald man near death. Not long after that, two redheads wearing fleece jackets and black stretch pants walked in and peered down into the pit. They are going to go home and give amazing head, Paul thought. Like a tadpole to water, or a turtle to the ocean after being born in a pit of sand, or a wobbly calf reaching its neck to the udder of its mother, a redhead knows how to give shockingly good head. They are attuned to it, as I am to moaning about my life.

Paul passionately believed that once you have suffered enough for telling your story it becomes worth telling. Otherwise just vanity, the lives of Brooklyn couples going on vacation in Tulum, unreal as tales of dragons. One may as well work in a cubicle and enter data and worry about balding if the alternative is to bring more of those stories to the world, he thought. The ambient music came to a lull in his headphones, and Paul could have sworn he overheard one of the college girls talking about a male stripper. Their lives, he imagined, are full of possibility. They do not care about the problems of the world, about men ruining everything with their selfish ambition and disgusting desires. Once, Paul thought, I had their brand of innocent promise, but now, sitting in a coffee shop where no one knew him, he could look at the clunky laptop in front of him and see that he had not written a word. The immensity of the universe seemed heavy, and his existence too light.

As he got up to leave Paul looked down into the pit and wondered if his neck would crack upon impact, or if there would be a period of labored groans. To hear the horrified screams of the college girls would be agony, he thought, thinking how it might sound close to their climaxing, which would only make him yearn, he thought, right to the very end.

—

After a barista with soft eyes poured his black iced tea, Paul sat in the back on a Friday evening. He'd been kicked out of his apartment. His building manager had knocked and asked if she could show the place. They were upping the rent. He couldn't afford it, but he didn't know where he would live next. For the time being he had no choice but to say, Yep, no problem, then leave, taking the trash with him. Outside he'd touched the lid of the industrial bin, and now in the coffee shop he had thoughts of giving other patrons terminal diseases. A new pack of college girls accumulated to his right, at a table for four. They came in a trickle, one with overwhelming curves, and after that a well-dressed one, and after that two sportier versions of youth, both fierce in athletic wear, looking as though they had stayed up drinking the night before and had ended up in bed with their boyfriends, who'd gotten into a brawl while defending their ladies' respective honors after hearing that a douche from a dorm across campus had said their girl had a great ass.

In the coffee shop Paul kept the ambient sounds in his headphones loud enough to prevent eavesdropping. Somehow, he knew, the college girls would know what he was thinking and call the authorities. Instead of playing his fantasy role-playing video game, Paul read an article about a man in Toronto, who in his thirties lived with his parents. The man did not want to buy a house, he said in the article, as he did not want to be bogged down with a mortgage. He spent all his money on high-end liquor and hotels and flights to Europe and Asia. He said his parents were devout Christians, so there were drawbacks to the arrangement, like when he brought a girl home—but, the man added, his parents got over it.

The article made Paul glad he'd never subjected his parents to such embarrassments. Still, he agonized in the coffee shop, thinking about how his lady was gone and he hadn't told his aging mom and dad. Maybe, Paul thought, he could keep on making excuses for why she never came to holiday functions and eventually they would tacitly agree to never bring her up.

A woman walked into the back room of the coffee shop. Paul looked at her unabashedly, like everyone else. She had crystal-blue eyes and wore a short skirt. She sat down across from an older gentleman with gray hair. Then came another, in a form-fitting dress made of soft green material. Then came a full-figured one, with straight black hair and a flowing diaphanous top and tight jeans, who sat by the one in the low-cut green dress. All these people would not be with Paul, that weekend or ever. What would he do then, as a bald white bearded man in a Rust Belt city? He could only think of going to the lake, the bookstore, and the coffee shop. Over and over, that trio on a loop. Jealous blood shot through Paul's veins at the

sight of the bald man, wearing
basketball shorts and a sweatshirt,
sitting across from the one in the form-
fitting green dress with the back cut in a
half-moon shape. What had he done to
convince her? What words in what
sequence did he use?

Paul rubbed his head and felt the
rubbery spot. The night before Tyler had
gotten out of bed as his wife dozed. The
hair on the side of Tyler's head had
grown long. Almost a week had passed
since the last time he buzzed it, so that
when he hooked the tinted shades onto
his glasses and wore one of his neon
shirts from Walmart, he looked more like
a hick from Southern Indiana than an
interventional radiologist with a salary of
over half a million dollars a year and a
Jewish wife and a Chilean surgeon for a
father-in-law. Tyler, bald on top, had
received a video clip from a woman he
used to see in Chicago. She played with
a dildo, sliding it in and out of her ass,
and moaned Tyler's name. It had been
his request. Tyler's second baby slept in
another room, a mobile spinning above
her head. All the while Mike's head
looked shiny after he'd shaved the sides
that morning. His Christian girlfriend had
waxed his back the night before, but
she'd left the rugs of hair on his legs and
the prickly stuffing around his balls and

prick. He didn't care, and his Christian
girlfriend had never known anything
different. Mike, done with a day of
programming, sat at home in the
suburbs on his red velvet couch, eating
a meal of venison and ramen noodles
washed down with a beer after getting
head from his Christian girlfriend. She
did not complain when he didn't
reciprocate. He'd had a hard day
coding, setting up their future.

Paul drank his tea, the ice melting into
the sugar, his name scribbled on the
side of the clear plastic cup. Two
toddlers walked in with their father. They
scrambled onto chairs so they could
peer over the ledge and down into the
hole. The father was blessed with a full
head of thick hair, the kind a sergeant in
the army would have and not think twice
about. To that man, Paul imagined,
having hair was like having a finger or
an elbow. One of the college girls
sneezed, loud like a woman's sneeze,
and Paul thought of how the barista with
the chestnut skin had known his order,
but it was nothing more than
transactional, the way she rang him up;
then he thought of the brown barista
with the dark-rimmed glasses who
looked like a star of the videos Paul
watched while perched with one foot on
the edge of the bathtub. She never

served him, so they didn't have a connection. Then he thought of the blonde in line with her father. She wore jean shorts and a white crop top that stopped halfway down her slim torso, a silver belly-button ring accentuating her tan stomach. But Paul was not a twenty-year-old with a motorcycle and a good job in construction. He could not take her on secret trips to Florida that she would consider equal to going to Rome. Paul sat alone in the coffee shop by the window where the sunlight persisted. Light streamed onto his black laptop, and for a few minutes he internally discussed whether he should think of it as a win-win, that he could be inside while at the same time getting a tan. He thought a browner scalp made him look less bald, but he could never take anything as a win-win. He worried that if his laptop got too warm from the sunlight an element would overheat, and that would threaten its main function, as a system for his fantasy video game. Another college student came into the back room. She sat at the long table everyone else in the back seemed reluctant to sit at for fear that a larger group would walk in and wordlessly demand deference. Paul was sure she would not acquiesce to anyone, with her blue eyes like a wolf's, heavy makeup, black hair, and lips that looked too plump, like they commanded too much attention. She wore black spandex pants and a Bucks jersey knotted at the waist. She looked straight ahead as she walked, in a way that said she knew men looked at her but she had no intention of looking back. She plopped down a cloth bag with brown leather straps, an MCAT study workbook and sheets of paper jammed inside. Her plans went beyond the confines of the coffee shop. Someday she'd come back and demand that someone make her another cappuccino. The previous had been, as she said, just too milky.

Returning to his fantasy video game in the coffee shop made for him, Paul began to daydream about a world where his lady's Russian friends were wrong, the osteopaths with husbands who worked as whiskey salesmen and botany professors. In comparison to them, Paul looked like he'd grown up on a pig farm. His jeans did not taper at his ankles. Unlike theirs, his went wide to accommodate his big legs. But in his daydream Paul was like them, perhaps the director of a hemp company. No longer did he work at a soulless job near the fairgrounds in the Wisconsin suburbs. He made a lot of money and could, after biking to get there, order expertly at a tapas restaurant in the

JEFFREY ELLINGER

Ukrainian Village. Paul shook his head
and looked down, then up in dismay.
Remind me again what the point of
being alive is? To buy a product? To talk
to someone? To eat?

The world cannot be saved, Paul knew.
The novel on balding had to be finished,
and if no one ever wrote it questions
would remain, like what would happen
to the two bald men? Would Tyler see
his hundredth pair of breasts? Would
Mike get to criticize a woman he'd met
in passing at a tech meetup for having a
nose one-sixteenth of an inch too long?
They'd never become physical if Paul
went to sleep, but that's what happened
at the apartment, where he did not
dream, and in the morning woke to the
biting of his own tongue.